力得文化
Leader Culture

Lead your way. Be your own leader!

力得文化
Leader Culture

Lead your way. Be your own leader!

力得文化
Leader Culture

時尚
秘書英語

Secretary/Assistant/
Marketing/ PR English in the
Fashion Industry

黃予辰◎著

實現TOP時尚特助、公關、行銷夢！
Boss必看　新鮮人入行必備！

規劃【秘書特助】、【秘書特助行銷公關】雙篇，
行政安排、品牌行銷、媒體公關、活動執行等等情境流程 一次收錄！
取得在職專業知識＋提升英文能力的4大秘訣：

秘書特助工作的內容介紹：一窺秘書特助、行銷、公關都在做什麼！
職場上實況對談一問三答：提供專業對答，同時提升英文聽說能力！
秘書特助對答技巧小提點：高手提點口語表達的技巧，加深印象！
秘書特助經驗不藏私分享：工作TIPS大公開，專業知識立即上手！

MP3

本書是專為有志進入時尚界的學生，或是欲轉職的上班族所設計的參考英文書籍。第一大章節的內容設計宗旨為協助剛入行的菜鳥助理更快融入時尚界。透過 24 種狀況問答與解析的方式，補足時尚界所必備的字彙與常識，面對任何突發狀況都能快速找到應對方式。第二大章則針對時尚界的行銷與公關兩大主題，透過生活化與實用的問答方式，來瞭解時尚品牌的育成、時尚界的行銷技巧和活動企劃、歐美時尚秀與公關工作的 know-how 等。另外還貼心附上文章解析，並揀選出內文的精華單字，讓讀者能夠洞悉時尚界的內幕，同時補足相關的英語備戰力，與國際時尚界零距離。

黃予辰

時尚精品業相關職務乍看像是光鮮亮麗的工作，但要在競爭激烈的環境中，要做得好、做得稱職，並不容易。《時尚秘書英語》一書不僅讓我們有機會一窺秘書特助和老闆間的互動，也能看得到行銷、公關為了推廣產品，和媒體、藝人、設計師之間的交流；其中還能聽到店家談論衣服的材質，或是特助向廠商確認布料顏色、介紹推出的指彩色系，這些都是在閱讀本書時，讀者能額外學到的字彙和專業知識。

現在就跟著本書，戴上耳機，播放 MP3，一同身歷其境，體驗時尚精品業的 48 種情境，同時提升英文「聽」、「說」的能力！

編輯部敬上

編者序

editor's words

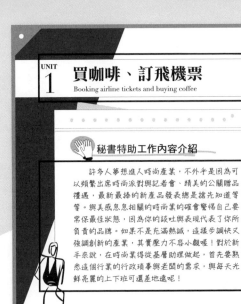

UNIT **1** 買咖啡、訂飛機票
Booking airline tickets and buying coffee

👋 秘書特助工作內容介紹

　　許多人夢想進入時尚產業，不外乎是因為可以頻繁出席時尚派對與記者會、精美的公關贈品禮遇，最新最捧的新產品發表總是搶先知道等等。與美感息息相關的時尚業的確驚惕自己要常保最佳狀態，因為你的談吐與表現代表了你所負責的品牌。如果不是充滿熱誠，這進步調快又強調創新的產業，其實壓力不容小覷喔！對於新手來說，在時尚業得從基層助理做起，首先要熟悉這個行業的行政瑣事與老闆的需求，與每天光鮮亮麗的上下班可還差地遠呢！

10

每單元以工作內容為開頭，並有淺顯易懂的介紹，有助馬上進入學習情境！

UNIT 1 ◆ 買咖啡、訂飛機票

🎧 職場上實況對談的一問二答　　◎ Track 01

❶ 秘書特助篇

首先我們先來搞定老闆喜歡的咖啡口味、行程報告和住宿安排吧！以下是菜鳥特助實習生 Amilia 與時尚業主管 Ms. Kylie 的問答：

❷ 秘書特助行銷公關篇

Question 1
Ⓐ **Ms. Kylie, how would you like your coffee?**
請問您喝咖啡的習慣是什麼？

Possible answer 1
Ⓚ Black Coffee with milk, please.
請給我黑咖啡和牛奶。

Possible answer 2
Ⓚ 1 cream, and 2 sugars, please.
請幫我加一份奶精和兩份糖。

特別設計工作情境的一問二答，邊聽 MP3，邊透過中英對照文字，同步提升職場英語「聽」、「說」能力！

早上 9 點鐘準時接您。這裡有聞名世界的龍蝦酒吧和燒烤，讓您在會議的前一天晚上，能夠充分的放鬆和享受。

特助行銷公關篇

▌特助補給單字
brief v. 簡要提報
itinerary n. 旅行計畫
accommodation n. 住宿

13

每問答後皆整理出關鍵單字，輕鬆累積字彙量！

秘書特助對答技巧提點

How would you like your coffee?

➔ 這句的情境比較適合一般公司會提供的研磨咖啡機或是全自動咖啡機啦。除了黑咖啡以外只會提供糖跟奶精的這種狀況，你還可以用上面的問句來詢問對方要幾包糖或奶精。其他常見的回答方式還有「double-double」，即是糖跟奶精都雙份的意思。

Noted. I have booked the Ritz Carlton for you since it is right next to the convention center you will be going to the next morning. May I book a spa treatment for you to help you refresh for the next day?

➔ Noted 是 note 的過去式，代表接收到老闆的指示，並且已經筆記下來了。Book 當名詞的時候是書本的意思，當成動詞使用就是預訂的意思。如：Book an appointment（預訂會面）、I would like to book a hotel room on January 1st.（我想在一月一號訂房。）

貼心地詢問是否需要 Spa 的課程是典型的特助工作，不只要注意工作上的效率，替老闆更全面性的著想出差行程是否太過緊湊，甚至是老闆的習慣喜好都得兼顧，讓工作品質更提升才是稱職喔！

14

精闢提點一問二答的應答技巧，教你講對英文，職場英語口說不出糗！

秘書特助經驗分享

特助的工作很繁瑣，但無形中也讓你接觸很多不同領域的事物。上司談話的內容與指導你的部分是很值得學習的！跟著業界的頂尖人才，你才能看到這個產業真正的樣貌。

從之前問答出現的：1 PM flight will be more ideal since I would like to check in as soon as I arrive, and the accommodations? 這個問題中，漸漸了解你必須學會旅程安排該注意的大小事，同時去感受老闆願意從容的出差模式，而不是塞滿行程速戰速決的旅程。詢問住宿代表主管在意這方面的安排，而 accommodation 的選擇性當然不只是 hotel 而已，像是 serviced apartment（飯店式公寓）或者是 self-catered（附設廚房）都是可以納入考慮的選項。

MEMO

15

看秘書特助不藏私分享，一次吸收專業知識與工作小訣竅，學英文，專業也同步提升！

❶ 秘書特助篇

❷ 秘密特助行銷公關篇

目次 CONTENTS

PART 2 秘書特助行銷公關篇

Marketing/public relations job profiles in the fashion industry

PART **1**

秘書特助篇

Secretary/administrator job profiles
in the fashion industry

買咖啡、訂飛機票

Booking airline tickets and buying coffee

 秘書特助工作內容介紹

　　許多人夢想進入時尚產業，不外乎是因為可以頻繁出席時尚派對與記者會、精美的公關贈品禮遇，最新最棒的新產品發表總是搶先知道等等。與美感息息相關的時尚業的確會警惕自己要常保最佳狀態，因為你的談吐與表現代表了你所負責的品牌。如果不是充滿熱誠，這樣步調快又強調創新的產業，其實壓力不容小覷喔！對於新手來說，在時尚業得從基層助理做起，首先要熟悉這個行業的行政瑣事與老闆的需求，與每天光鮮亮麗的上下班可還差地遠呢！

職場上實況對談的一問二答　 Track 01

首先我們先來搞定老闆喜歡的咖啡口味、行程報告和住宿安排吧！以下是菜鳥特助實習生 Amilia 與時尚業主管 Ms. Kylie 的問答：

Question 1

🅰 **Ms. Kylie, how would you like your coffee?**
請問您喝咖啡的習慣是什麼？

Possible answer 1

🅚 Black Coffee with milk, please.
請給我黑咖啡和牛奶。

Possible answer 2

🅚 1 cream, and 2 sugars, please.
請幫我加一份奶精和兩份糖。

Question 2

🅚 **You can start briefing me on my business travel itinerary.**
你可以開始報告我的商務行程了。

Possible answer 1

🅐 Of course, let's start with flight arrangements. I checked online and got a few flight schedule options for your business trip to Hong Kong. Would you

11

prefer to arrive in the morning or in the afternoon?

好的，那麼我們從您的航班開始。為了您的香港出差之旅，我在網路上查了一些航班時刻表，你會想在早上或在下午到達？

Possible answer 2

🅰 Yes, as for your business trip to Hong Kong, the travel agency has confirmed a 9 AM flight and a 1 PM flight. Which one do you prefer?

好的，關於您要到香港出差，我已經跟旅行社確認過有上午 9 點的航班和下午 1 點航班，請問您屬意哪一個航班？

Question 3

🅚 **The 1 PM flight will be more ideal since I would like to check in as soon as I arrive, and the accommodation?**

下午一點的班機會比較理想，我希望能夠一下飛機就能辦理入房。那住宿方面呢**？**

Possible answer 1

🅰 Noted. I have booked the Ritz Carlton for you since it is right next to the convention center you will be going to the next morning. May I book a spa treatment for you to help you refresh the next day?

我了解了，我已經為您預訂了麗思卡爾頓酒店，因為它就在您第二天早上要過去的會展中心旁邊。另外我可以幫您預訂

Spa 按摩療程，以消除旅程的疲勞嗎？

Possible answer 2

🅐 As for the accommodation, it will be the Shangri-La. I will have a car ready to pick you up at 9 o'clock in the morning. With their world famous lobster bar and grill, you will be able to relax and enjoy your night before the meeting.

關於住宿，我訂了香格里拉飯店，也已經預備好專車在隔天早上 9 點鐘準時接您。這裡有聞名世界的龍蝦酒吧和燒烤，讓您在會議的前一天晚上，能夠充分的放鬆和享受。

▌特助補給單字

brief *v.* 簡要提報

itinerary *n.* 旅行計畫

accommodation *n.* 住宿

秘書特助對答技巧提點

How would you like your coffee?

➲ 這句的情境比較適合一般公司會提供的研磨咖啡機或是全自動咖啡機機。除了黑咖啡以外只會提供糖跟奶精的這種狀況，你還可以用上面的問句來詢問對方要幾包糖或奶精。其他常見的回答方式還有 「double-double」，即是糖跟奶精都雙份的意思。

Noted. I have booked the Ritz Carlton for you since it is right next to the convention center you will be going to the next morning. May I book a spa treatment for you to help you refresh for the next day?

➲ Noted 是 note 的過去式，代表接收到老闆的指示，並且已經筆記下來了。Book 當名詞的時候是書本的意思，當成動詞使用就是預訂的意思。如：Book an appointment（預訂會面）、I would like to book a hotel room on January 1st.（我想在一月一號訂房。）

貼心地詢問是否需要 Spa 的課程是典型的特助工作，不只要注意工作上的效率，替老闆更全面性地著想出差行程是否太過緊湊，甚至是老闆的習慣喜好都得兼顧，讓工作品質更提升才是稱職喔！

秘書特助經驗分享

　　特助的工作很繁瑣，但無形中也讓你接觸很多不同領域的事物。上司談話的內容與指導你的部分是很值得學習的！跟著業界的頂尖人才，你才能看到這個產業真正的樣貌。

　　從之前問答出現的：1 PM flight will be more ideal since I would like to check in as soon as I arrive, and the accommodations? 這個問題中，漸漸了解你必須學會旅程安排該注意的大小事，同時去感受老闆屬意從容的出差模式，而不是塞滿行程速戰速決的旅程。詢問住宿代表主管在意這方面的安排，而 accommodation 的選擇性當然不只是 hotel 而已，像是 serviced apartment（飯店式公寓）或者是 self-catered（附設廚房）都是可以納入考慮的選項。

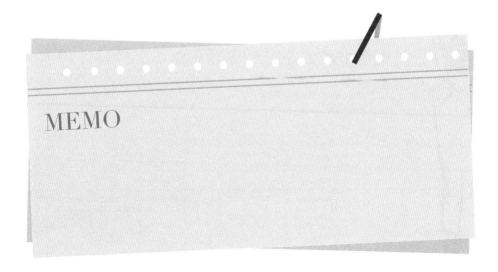

MEMO

電話接聽與問題處理

Dealing with telephone calls and inquiries

 ## 秘書特助工作內容介紹

你有沒有發現，主管級的人物，很少會自己接聽電話。如果是待過辦公室的上班族都知道，打來公司的電話，很多都是推銷業務，如果主管都一一應酬，恐怕沒時處理公事了。所以如何電話接應與適當地處理問題，是你首要學會的工作（Screening all incoming calls is your first task as being an assistant.）。你得多花時間，理解公司處理事情的流程、老闆重視的人事物是哪些、各部門的聯絡窗口是哪位，甚至是公司進行中的案子……等等，你才能做好你份內的工作。

職場上實況對談的一問二答 Track 02

時尚產業重視的是視覺形象與潮流，這樣的產業需要同行一起響應，再加上媒體的幫助，才能相輔相成。很多時候的交流，除了 e-mail 之外，電話聯絡會更有誠意，因此電話接聽上該注意的禮貌與相關用語，你得好好鑽研。以下其他企業的公關代表 PR 與特助 Amilia 之間的問答：

Question 1

PR **Hi Amilia, this is Grace from the Taipei Times. We are preparing a topic about successful career women to give our readers some insights on the fashion industry. And we are very interested in interviewing Ms. Kylie. Do you think I can talk to her and discuss it?**

愛蜜莉亞妳好，我是台北時報的葛瑞絲，我們正在做關於成功職業女性的專題，好讓我們的讀者更深入瞭解時尚界。我們很希望可以專訪凱莉女士，你覺得我是否可以跟她聊聊這件事呢？

Possible answer 1

A Hi, Grace. This is Amilia Huang. It's so good to hear from you. Ms. Kylie will be thrilled to talk to you about the interview. She will be free after this meeting in about 20 minutes. Would you like to come over for a cup of coffee or perhaps have lunch with us?

葛瑞絲您好，我是愛蜜莉亞・黃，聽到妳的聲音真開心。凱莉女士一定會很樂意跟您討論專訪的事情。她再 20 分鐘後就會開完這個會，之後就有空了。你願意過來喝杯咖啡，或者我們和一起吃午飯嗎？

Possible answer 2

🅰 Hi, Grace. Amilia Huang speaking. How are you? Ms. Kylie couldn't stop talking about your last report about us. It helped us gain more than 3,000 followers on Facebook. We couldn't be happier. Would you just hold on a minute before I transfer your call to her?

嗨，葛瑞絲，我是愛蜜莉亞・黃，妳最近好嗎？凱莉小姐對於您上一篇對我們的報導，真是滿意得不得了。它讓我們在臉書上多了 3000 多位追隨者，我們超開心的。請妳給我一點時間，我馬上幫您轉接給她。

Question 2

🅿🆁 Hi, this is Brianna Lee. I am calling for the cooperation in the art exhibit in April. Since the topic of our exhibit is about the spring in a botanical garden, we would like to know how you are planning to participate in this activity?

您好，我是碧艾娜・李，我打電話過來是為了四月的藝術

展覽合作。由於我們展覽的主題是關於植物園中的春天，我們想知道你們怎麼樣配合這次的活動？

Possible answer 1

Ⓐ Hi, Brianna. This is Amilia Huang. Thank you for calling. About the art exhibit in April, we are thrilled to be a part of it. As a matter of fact, we were just in a meeting talking about our action plan. We have a great marketing team that can provide assistance to the event newsletters and marketing materials such as invitations and pamphlets.

碧艾娜，您好，我是愛蜜莉亞·黃，謝謝您打電話過來。關於四月的藝術展覽，我們很高興能夠參與其中。事實上，我們剛才在開會談論我們的行動企劃。我們有一個強大的行銷團隊，針對新聞稿和行銷輔銷物也許我們可以幫的上忙，如邀請函和介紹小冊子等。

Possible answer 2

Ⓐ Hello, Brianna. We were just talking about the art exhibit a minute ago. I am so glad that you called. As to the topic of the spring in a botanical garden, we can support you with our newest collection of women's clutches. The flower embroidery and the lightweight materials will blend in with the rest of the art works. What do you think?

您好，碧艾娜，我很高興您打電話過來。我們剛剛正在討論

這個展覽呢！關於植物園中的春季這個主題，我想我們可以提供我們最新的女用手提包。有著花卉刺繡和輕質材料等特色，可以跟其他藝術裝置完美融合在一起。您覺得怎麼樣呢？

特助補給單字

botanical *adj.* 植物的

exhibit *n.* 展覽

clutch *n.* 手拿包

 ## 秘書特助對答技巧提點

Ms. Kylie's office. This is Amilia Huang speaking.

➲ 說出自己負責的主管辦公室，這也是常見的電話禮儀。你有發覺嗎？在電話上的溝通因為不是面對面，所以愛蜜莉亞會禮貌地說出自己的全名。而這樣的打招呼方式常見的有這兩種：

1. Amilia Huang speaking. How may I help you today?

   （我是愛蜜莉亞‧黃，我今天可以怎樣協助您呢？）

2. This is Amilia Huang. It's so great to hear from you.

   （我是愛蜜莉亞‧黃，很高興聽到你的聲音。）

   注意：在電話中完整地說出自己的全名，是專業與負責任的態度，請筆記！

We can support you with our newest collection of women's clutches.

● support 是支持的意思，在這裡的用法是「提供」的意思。
例：We support the global marathon with 1000 bottles of mineral water and sports drinks.（我們免費提供全球馬拉松一千瓶礦泉水與運動飲料。）

秘書特助經驗分享

　　幫主管過濾各種電話，可以有效地提升辦公的效率。偶爾仍會有些重要的訊息需要傳達與請主管回電，因此良好的 message taking（電話留言）是你份內的工作。首先，電話響的時候，你要儘快接電話。留言的內容你要記下：name of the caller（對方姓名）、name of the business（公司行號）、phone number（回電電話）、purpose of the call（目的）並 repeat to make sure the message is accurate（複誦確認內容無誤）。

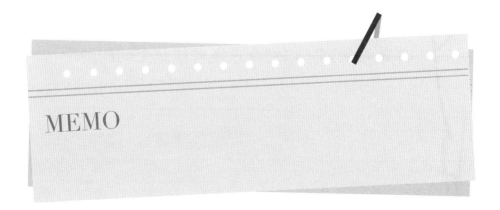

MEMO

行政工作處理

Performing administrative duties

 秘書特助工作內容介紹

　　助理的庶務之二就是負責與主管相關的行政工作，比方說請假程序的辦理、追蹤專案的進度與其相關的文書工作等等，都是由特助一手包辦。行政工作也需要優越的電腦技能和部門之間的協調（Administrative activities also include extensive computer skills and the coordination between departments.）。也許內容繁瑣，但公司越大就越需要層層關卡的審核，以確保公司最大的利益。這些程序雖然耗費時間，卻不能馬虎，因此特助也要為主管留意簽呈的細節是否正確、簽呈的時效性或是程序的辦理是否周到，以避免日後可能發生的糾紛。

職場上實況對談的一問二答　 Track 03

公司內部通常只要牽涉到預算，就會需要透過簽呈的流程。預算越多，需要簽核的層級就越高。有時候辦大型活動會需要各部門協力合作，經常也會透過簽呈，讓各部門都瞭解活動的時間、地點與職責。接下來我們就透過特助 Amilia 與各部門 Marketing: Bobbie、Human Resources: Hailey 的問答，讓大家理解時尚業常見的行政業務吧！

Question 1

🅱 **Hello, Amilia. I have the memo and interdepartmental billing form for the PR event in *Castle Café*. Do you have a couple of minutes to take a look? There are a few things that we need to cooperate on and rehearse before planning further.**

你好，愛蜜莉亞，我帶了即將在*城堡咖啡館*舉辦的公關活動的備忘錄，還有跨部門的預算分配表。你有幾分鐘可以討論一下嗎？有幾件事情我們需要合作和預先排練，才能再做進一步的規劃。

Possible answer 1

🅰 Yes, of course, please have a seat. Let's see... So for the PR event, you will need Ms. Kylie to give a brief speech on the corporate vision as well as her participation in the lucky draw activity halfway

23

through the event. I don't think there will be a problem at all. I will write up a speech draft for her and discuss it with her and see if there is anything she would like to adjust for the event.

當然好啊，請坐。讓我來看一下……，所以你需要凱莉小姐在活動上簡短地闡述企業願景，以及參與活動中段的抽獎活動。我認為可行性很高，我會先擬她的演講稿，再跟她討論是否有需要調整的地方。

Possible answer 2

🅰 Hello, Bobbie. I will be more than happy to take a look. Ok, I think the rundown of the PR event is impeccable, and we will do everything to support this event. However, for the interdepartmental billing form, I have a few questions to ask. As for the catering charges, I have to double-check with Ms. Kylie about the number of guests we plan to invite, and then we can split the cost more logically, would you agree?

您好巴比，我很樂意喔。好的，我覺得公關活動的流程幾乎無可挑剔，我們會盡一切努力去支持這項活動。然而，跨部門的費用分攤方式，我倒是有幾個問題要問。餐飲收費的部分，我會先跟凱莉小姐確認我們要邀請的賓客人數，這樣一來我們可以更合理地分攤費用，不知您是否同意呢？

Question 2

🕪 **Hi, Amilia. This is Hailey from Human Resources. I just received Ms. Kylie's vacation request form from you. Since the vacation exceeds 10 days, she might have to list all the contact windows of her current projects in case of emergency.**

嗨，愛蜜莉亞，我是人力資源部的海利。我剛剛收到了凱莉女士的休假申請。所有的文件看起來沒什麼問題。不過因為這是超過 10 天的休假，她可能得列出目前專案接洽中所有的聯絡窗口，以避免緊急需要聯絡的情況。

Possible answer 1

🅐 Hello, Hailey. Thank you for taking the time to process the vacation request on such short notice.

您好海利，感謝您在這麼短的時間內，抽空處理好凱莉小姐的休假申請。

Possible answer 2

🅐 Hello, Hailey. I am so glad that the request went through. As for contact information, I will update them with Ms. Kylie and send them to you as soon as possible.

您好海利，我很高興請假程序已經通過了。至於聯繫窗口的部分，我會跟凱莉女士取得最新的版本，也會盡快發一份給你。

特助補給單字

bill *v.* 開帳單

vision *n.* 視野

draft *n.* 草稿

 秘書特助對答技巧提點

You will need Ms. Kylie to give a brief speech on the corporate vision as well as her participation in the lucky draw activity halfway through the event.

⊃ Participate 參與，常用於參與討論的或是活動，如：You need to <u>participate in</u> the meeting in order to impress your superior.（你得積極地在會議上發言，才能讓你的上司對你印象深刻。）

I have to double-check with Ms. Kylie about the number of guests that we plan to invite, and then we can split the cost more logically, would you agree?

⊃ Double-check 再次確認，這是很常見的用法口語用法。例句有：I have to <u>double-check</u> the time of the Sunday brunch; I will check my agenda and get back to you as soon as possible.（我得再次確認週日早午餐的時間，在看過我的行事曆之後，我會盡快回覆您的。）

⊃ Split the cost 分攤費用，相關應用：

Let's rent a car while we travel and we can <u>split the</u> <u>cost</u>.（我們旅行的時候來租車吧，這樣還可以一起分攤費用。）

 秘書特助經驗分享

　　特助在擬簽呈的時候，除了目標要清楚，也要確實列出所有會簽的部門，這樣在檢討績效以及責任歸屬的時候就能一目瞭然。比方說財務部在計算年度盈餘的時候，如果有爭議，就可以在簽呈上看出行銷或是業務部做了哪些促銷活動。而品牌效益如果有呈現出來，比方說回購率增加或是粉絲團人數的進步，也能將毛利的犧牲看成廣告投資。

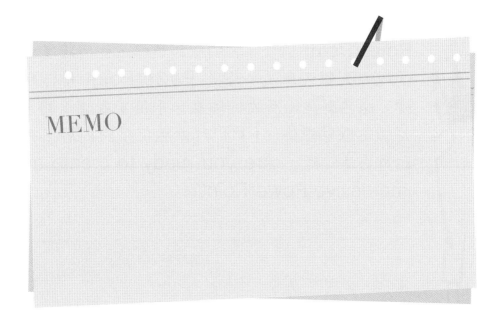

MEMO

簡報製作

Making PowerPoint for presentations

 秘書特助工作內容介紹

　　作為一個特助，Microsoft Word 方面的文書處理能力是必備的。Word、Excel 和 PowerPoint 這三個軟體的操作請務必要加強。首先你的打字速度要快，因為會議記錄與 e-mail 的往來，都要分秒必爭，正確無誤。再來，基本的預算和業績的加總與分析，通常是透過 Excel 來處理，才能簡單明瞭。最後是 PowerPoint（PPT）的簡報製作，如何將畫面呈現的美觀又專業，除了 PowerPoint 操作熟練，還要有強而有力的論點、十足掌握聽眾的喜好與美感等條件。PPT 可以強化演說內容，讓聽眾更專心聽。 Are you ready to create an impressive PowerPoint?

職場上實況對談的一問二答　 Track 04

好的 PowerPoint 可以協助聽眾瞭解複雜的概念，無論是透過圖像或是重點分析。PPT 不求花俏，越簡單越能清楚表達想闡述的論點。時尚業更是追求視覺的呈現，每張 PPT 的字型、大小與顏色都要一致。其他 PowerPoint 檔製作的技巧，就透過以下特助 Amilia 與 Ms. Kylie 的問答告訴你們吧！

Question 1

🅚 **Amilia, how are we doing on the PowerPoint slides for the lecture on market trends? Am I not going to get them on the day of my presentation?**

愛蜜莉亞，市場發展趨勢講座的 **PPT** 做得怎樣了？我不會要在我的演講當天才拿得到吧？

Possible answer 1

🅐 Of course not, Ms. Kylie. I am working on the final touches of the PowerPoint design. I am done with the entire wording except the take-home message.

凱莉小姐，當然不是這樣，我正在為 PPT 的設計進行最後的潤色。除了給聽眾的一句話，其餘報告中的文字都完成了。

Possible answer 2

🅐 Absolutely not. I apologize for not bringing them to you sooner. Now I am just deciding between two font styles and proofreading the slides right now. I actually would like to discuss the ratio of keywords and images with you.

絕對不是，很抱歉我沒有早點把它們交給您。現在我正在為兩種字體樣式間作決定，以及進行校對。其實我想跟您討論關鍵字和圖像的比例。

Question 2

🅚 **Amilia, I would like to talk to you about the PowerPoint slides for our new brand proposal. White background and black texts are probably the best bet, but I personally think color is a motivator and increases comprehension, especially in the fashion industry. What's your point of view?**

嗨！愛蜜莉亞，我想和你談談我們的新品牌提案的 **PPT** 檔案。我知道白色背景和黑色文字可能是最安全的選擇，但我個人認為顏色是一種動力，還可以增加理解，尤其在時裝界更是如此。對於色系妳的觀點是什麼呢？

Possible answer 1

🅐 I think warm colors do attract more attention, so we could try that on some of the key words, and cool colors will work better for backgrounds. We need to consider the location of the presentation.

我覺得溫暖的顏色的確比較容易引起注目，所以我們可以嘗

試在部分的關鍵字，而 PPT 的背景則是比較適合採用冷色系。我們需要考慮的演講的地方。

Possible answer 2

🅐 Well, I do think black and white are dull, so I was thinking we can use the color of our logo and create the background color, but keep the rest of the templates straight and simple. I want our PPT slides to be tasteful and focus only on the new brands.

嗯，我覺得只用黑色與白色有點過於平淡，所以我想我們可以用我們商標的顏色來建立一個背景設計，但其他部分就盡量簡單素雅。我希望 PPT 檔案可以看起來雅緻，只把注意力放在新品牌的介紹上。

特助補給單字

proofread *v.* 校對

ratio *n.* 比例

text *n.* 文字

motivator *n.* 動力

comprehension *n.* 理解

秘書特助對答技巧提點

I am done with the entire wording except the take-home message.

○ Take-home message 是整個演講的核心精神，也可以是講者希望聽者帶回家思考的問題，或是將 speech 濃縮成一句話，為聽眾作總結的意思。

White background and black texts are probably the best bet, but I personally think color is a motivator and increases comprehension, especially in the fashion industry.

○ Motivator 這個名詞可以當作動力來源，或是一個促動的因素、句子或是人物。例 1：In an essay, a motivator is usually a sentence in the introduction that is used to retain the attention of the reader, so they are willing to continue reading the article.（在文章的引言中通常會有激勵句，它是用來留住讀者的注意力，讓他們願意繼續往下閱讀。）例 2：She is the motivator in all our group activities. Without her, people tend to slack off or leave the event early.（她是我們所有團體活動的動力；沒有她，人們往往會懈怠或提早離開。）

秘書特助經驗分享

　　時尚業的特助除了要會製作完美的 PPT 檔案，也要有簡報能力。請掌握五個重點，能讓你看起來自信滿滿。第一、熟悉簡報的內容：即使不盯著螢幕，你都知道下一張 slide 是什麼。第二、講話音量適中，切忌說話速度太快。第三、與聽眾維持眼神的交流。第四、融會貫通地說出你的論點，不要盯著 PPT 照念。最後，練習、練習再練習。

MEMO

會議通知與會議室準備
Announcing and organizing meetings

 秘書特助工作內容介紹

　　說到開會，其實都不是大家喜愛的工作項目之一，但卻不可否認開會的必要性。跨部門的資訊溝通、新品討論、活動企劃或行銷販售的方案，都需要大家共同討論，總結出最有效率的執行方案。時尚界看重的視覺美感、各種服裝配件的搭配與拍攝手法，以及每季的時尚訴求，都是整個時尚團隊集思廣益的成果。通常特助會負責召開會議、會議室的準備，以及會議記錄等工作。也許一開始你不會參與討論，但在這環境的耳濡目染之下，你會很快地成長。

職場上實況對談的一問二答 Track 05

特助除了會議前後要負責打理，也經常是召開會議以及協調開會時間的窗口。如果遇到會議時間更改或是會議內容有爭議的時候，你該如何處置呢？假設今天會議的主題是為了頂級婚紗品牌來打造相關議題，而與女性時尚雜誌合作專題，並探討婚禮籌備的流程。以下是 Amilia 與編輯部 Piper 之間的問答：

Question 1

P Hi, Amilia, this is Piper from editorial. I got the meeting notice of the "Wedding to-do list" article. I would like to add more topics on the meeting agenda. Since the to-do list is spread out in a year, every two months there are decisions and purchases to be made for the wedding. Perhaps we can break it down a little more.

嗨，愛蜜莉亞，我是編輯部的派普，我收到了「婚禮籌備流程表」文章的編輯會議通知。我想在討論議題裡補充一些標題。由於婚禮籌備的時間分布在一整年裡，每兩個月有該做的決策和婚禮採買，也許我們可以把流程分得更細。

Possible answer 1

A Hello, Piper. I totally agree with you. I am thinking there is something missing in the article. Thank you for pointing that out!

您好派普，我完全同意你的看法。我在想有文章內的確是少了點什麼，感謝您指出了這一點！

Possible answer 2

Ⓐ Hello, Piper. As for the list, I think an addition on the check list is all right, as long as the outline will not exceed more than half of the page. We need enough space for the wedding gown image to get exposure.

您好，派普，增加籌備清單的部分沒有問題，只要範圍不會超過頁面的一半以上。婚紗的形象需要足夠的空間曝光。

Question 2

Ⓟ Hi, Amilia. I know we have booked tomorrow morning for an editorial meeting. However, the digital production team has to upgrade the website and it seems that they might not be able to make it tomorrow. What do you think should we do?

嗨，愛蜜莉亞，我知道我們預訂明天早上的時間開編輯會議。然而，網路團隊目前正忙著網站升級，他們可能明天無法參加。你覺得應該怎麼辦才好？

Possible answer 1

Ⓐ Hi, Piper. Thank you for the notice. I will talk to the digital production team and check with them on their first availability since the bridal fashion week is coming in 2 weeks. We definitely want the article to appear online no later than that.

派普您好,謝謝你的通知。我會跟網路製作團隊聯絡,請他們提供最快能開會的時間,因為距離婚紗時裝週只剩兩個禮拜了。文章最慢也得在這個時間點前更新在網路上。

Possible answer 2

🅐 Hi, Piper. I guess we cannot afford the website to have any mishaps. Perhaps we can consult with the digital production team about the layout, illustration and digital effects at the very beginning of the meeting, then they can be back to the website construction right away after that.

派普您好,網站的確是不能有任何閃失。也許我們可以在會議一開始,就先請教網路製作團隊關於編排、插圖和特效方面的意見,討論完之後馬上讓他們回到網站更新的工作。

特助補給單字

editorial *adj.* 編輯的

spread out *ph.* 在某時間╱空間內展開

exceed *v.* 超過

availability *n.* 可利用性

mishap *n.* 災難

秘書特助對答技巧提點

Since the to-do list is spread out in a year, every two months there are decisions and purchases to be made for the wedding. Perhaps we can break it down a little more.

➲ Spread out 在某個時段或空間展開、散開的意思。例 1：The rumor about him getting fired has been spread out as soon as the secretary spilled the beans.（關於他被炒魷魚的傳聞，被秘書説溜嘴後就大肆傳了出去。）例 2：My boutiques are spread out 2 cities.（我的幾家精品店分布在兩個城市裡。）

I guess we cannot afford the website to have any mishaps.

➲ Afford 通常用來解釋「負擔得起」的意思。比方説：I cannot afford this trip to Hawaii because I just paid the down payment to my house.（我沒辦法負擔夏威夷的旅行，因為我才剛付了房子的頭期款。）但在上頁的文中是指「承受」的意思。例：Our team cannot afford another mistake since last season's sales was already below target.（我們的團隊無法承受再一次的打擊，因為上一季的銷售已經低於原先的目標。）

秘書特助經驗分享

　　一般來說可以透過 Outlook 系統召開會議通知，e-mail 中除了會議名稱與議題可以先列出來之外，還可以設定時間與會議室地點，再寄給所有的與會人即可。Outlook 的會議室通知還可以設定會議提醒，即使一週前就通知要開會，也可以透過系統在開會前一天做提醒通知。

MEMO

① 秘書特助篇

② 秘書特助行銷公關篇

UNIT 6 迎接訪客與引導至正確部門

Greeting visitors and redirect them to the proper departments

 秘書特助工作內容介紹

時尚產業幾乎每天都會與媒體、製造廠商以及客戶有密切的接觸。作為貼身助理需要幫助上司過濾對象，能代勞的就先處理，重要的約會再替主管安排時間進行。按照每個人的需求，正確分配到對應的單位，這樣進退應對的手腕是助理必要的技能（A good assistant knows how to greet visitors and callers, handle their inquiries and direct them to the appropriate department according to their needs.）。

職場上實況對談的一問二答　 Track 06

客戶來訪或是客服電話處理得當，絕對有助於提升公司整體形象。所以助理工作絕對不是面對上司而已，對外也是要面面俱到喔！以下是特助 Amilia 與訪客 Guest 交談之間可能出現的問答：

Question 1

Ⓖ **Hello, I am the sales representative of Taipei Advertising. I was hoping I can meet with Ms. Kylie to go over our newest campaign for social network advertising. I couldn't catch her on the phone, so I thought I could come over here to introduce myself.**

您好，我是台北廣告的業務。我希望我能和凱莉女士見一面，向她介紹我們公司推出最新的社群網站廣告方案。我沒辦法透過電話跟她取得聯繫，所以我就直接來這裡跟大家自我介紹了。

Possible answer 1

Ⓐ Thank you so much for coming. My name is Amilia. I am Ms. Kylie's personal assistant. If you would like, you may leave the advertising campaign materials with me and I will make sure Ms. Kylie gets them.

非常感謝您的光臨。我的名字是愛蜜莉亞，我是凱莉女士的

41

助理。如果您願意的話,您可以將廣告相關的資料給我,我
會確保凱莉女士收到這些文件。

Possible answer 2

A I see. Thank you for dropping by. My name is Amilia. Very pleased to meet you. I am afraid Ms. Kylie has stepped out for the day. If you would like, you can leave your contact information here, and I will try to schedule an appointment for you as soon as possible.

原來是這樣,謝謝您特地跑一趟。我的名字是愛蜜莉亞,很
高興認識您。不過凱莉小姐今天外出。如果方便的話,您可
以在這裡留下您的聯繫方式,我會盡快幫您安排會面的時
間。

Question 2

G Hi, I am calling to confirm the catering details for the new product release on Friday, but I accidently lost Mark's cell phone number. Can you give me Mark's extension?

你好,我打電話是為了確認這週五新產品發表會的餐飲細
節,但我不小心弄丟馬克的手機號碼,請問您可以給我他的
分機號碼嗎?

Possible answer 1

A Oh you must be Tim. This is Amilia. I am working

❶ 秘書特助篇

❷ 秘書特助行銷公關篇

very closely with Mark this week on the event. I am familiar with the catering requirements; you can actually confirm all the details with me because Mark is in a meeting right now.

您一定是提姆。我是愛蜜莉亞，我和馬克這禮拜因為活動的關係，有著很密切的合作。我非常瞭解餐飲方面的需求，您其實可以與我確認所有的細節，因為馬克現在正在開會。

Possible answer 2

🅐 Hello, this is Amilia. As for the new product release event, you can talk to the marketing team about the catering details. Mark should be in the office right now. Please hold while I transfer your call.

您好，我是愛蜜莉亞，關於新品發表會餐飲外燴的細節，您可以直接跟行銷團隊溝通。馬克現在應該在辦公室。請稍等一下，我幫您轉接。

▌ 特助補給單字

representative *n.* 代表

campaign *n.* 活動

social network *n.* 社群網站

step out *ph.* 外出

catering *n.* 承辦飲食

familiar *adj.* 熟悉的

transfer *v.* 轉接

秘書特助對答技巧提點

I was hoping I can meet with Ms. Kylie to go over our newest campaign for social network advertising.

⊃ Go over 這個片語代表的是從頭到尾清楚解釋的意思，也有溫習或是反覆思考的涵意。例：They went over the marketing budget and decided to put most of the expense on social network advertising.（他們仔細地再評估行銷預算，最後決定將大部分的預算投資在社群網站的廣告上面。）

Campaign 是活動的意思，而後面常用的介系詞是 for，例：We came up with the campaign for students; the buy one get one free campaign was a huge success.（我們構思的買一送一學生專案活動結果非常成功。）

I am familiar with the catering requirements.

⊃ Be familiar with ... 對某人某事非常通曉或熟悉。例：I am very familiar with the phenomenon of fashion industry, such as the style, glamour and how it reflects a person's value and individuality.（我很熟悉時尚產業的現象，比方說時尚的風格與魅力，以及它如何體現一個人的價值和個性。）

秘書特助經驗分享

　　將客戶引導至正確的公司部門，是特助必要的能力之一喔！一剛開始遇到絡繹不絕的客人與來電的詢問，一定會覺得很頭痛。不過，請有勇氣地克服這些問題，因為他們都可以幫你開拓更寬廣的未來，無論是媒體或廠商，跟他們溝通的過程當中你都會因此增長見聞。既然你已經被選中進入這個行業，就代表你有潛力在時尚業發展。不要氣餒，機會是屬於努力不懈與勇於面對挫折的人。深呼吸，仔細聽對方的需求並冷靜地做判斷，你身邊的上司與夥伴會指點你慢慢地進入狀況！加油吧！

MEMO

幫老闆安排時間

Appointment arrangements

 秘書特助工作內容介紹

　　貼身特助的另一個重要工作就是安排行程，將所有的約會時間安排妥當（Planning and scheduling meetings and appointments are important jobs of an executive assistant.）。一天上班時間就是八小時，如何替上司分辨輕重緩急，代為處理行政業務，讓重要的事情可以得到決策與執行辦法，是特助的職責所在（Helping your superior to manage workflow and meet deadline is also an assistant's job duties.），清楚地說明待辦事項與良好的時間控管，可以讓行程安排得更精準。這方面的溝通技巧需要清楚的邏輯與靈活的思路，如果你擁有以上的特質，那麼你在時尚產業之路將會很順利！

職場上實況對談的一問二答　 Track 07

每天特助的行程會報除了有提醒的作用，也有可能需要加進臨時的會議，或是因為某些事情而取消既定的行程。以下是針對時間安排，可能出現在是菜鳥特助實習生 Amilia 與時尚業主管 Ms. Kylie 之間的問答：

Question 1

🄚 I need to **squeeze** 20 minutes in to have a quick meeting with the new photographer by tomorrow.

我必須在明天前跟新來的攝影師開一個 **20** 分鐘的會議。

Possible answer 1

🄐 Let's see. The board meeting is from 9 to 10 o'clock, and then from 10 to 11, you will need to attend an advertising strategy meeting with the Marketing Department. There is also a lunch meeting with the editors at the plaza, so you will need to head out no later than 11:30. If 11:00 o'clock sounds good for you, I will call him right away to set it up.

我來看看，董事會是 9 到 10 點，而從 10 到 11 點行銷部召開的廣告策略會議，您也需要出席。之後是與編輯群在廣場飯店的午餐會議，所以您需要在 11 時 30 分前出發。如果您願意在 11 點跟攝影師開會，我會馬上跟他聯絡並跟他約好時間。

Possible answer 2

Ⓐ You are totally swamped from 9 to 3. However, after 3 you are going to the plaza to check out the location for the annual year-end party. You will have a window of 30 minutes before the conference call with Mr. Lee, the interior decorator at 5 o'clock. Perhaps I can make a reservation at the plaza café for your meeting with the photographer?

您從早上 9 點至下午 3 點的行程是完全排滿的。而 3 點後您得去廣場飯店看年終舞會的場地。在 5 點與室內設計師的電話會議之前，您會有 30 分鐘的空檔。也許我能幫您在廣場飯店附設的咖啡廳預約，好讓您與攝影師見面？

Question 2

Ⓚ I am stuck in traffic. Can you push all my schedules back by half an hour?

我碰到大塞車，你能把我所有的行程全部往後移半個小時嗎？

Possible answer 1

Ⓐ No problem. Your first meeting is with our team. Perhaps I can postpone that meeting till much later today, so that the rest of your schedule won't be affected.

沒問題。您今天第一個行程是我們的內部會議，或許我可以將它延後到今天晚點開會，這樣你其餘的排程就不會受到影響。

Possible answer 2

Ⓐ Don't worry. I will see what I can do. Your first meeting is with the fabric supplier. However, this is a 2-hour meeting. We probably could manage to go through all the subjects in time even if the meeting is delayed for 30 minutes. As for the next meeting, I will inform them to be aware of a possible delay.

不要擔心，我來看看能怎麼安排。第一個會議對象是布料供應商。然而這個會議預定是 2 小時，我想即使會議被延後 30 分鐘，我們還是有辦法在時間內解決所有議題。至於接下來的會議，我會先告知他們可能會有延後開會的狀況。

■ 特助補給單字

squeeze *v.* 擠壓

head out *ph.* 出發

swamp *v.* 忙得不可開交

annual *adj.* 一年一度

fabric *n.* 布料

秘書特助對答技巧提點

I will call him right away to set it up.

⊃ Set something up 這個片語代表著設置、成立的意思。Set up something 這樣的用法也是正確的！所以這句話也可以用 I will call him right away to <u>set up</u> the meeting. 來表達。 Set someone up 是一個特殊用法，將某人放在 set up 這個片語之中，有著口語的 match making 的涵義在。也就是說介紹或是替某人作媒的意思。Are you going to set me up with your coworker?（你會介紹你的同事給我認識嗎？）

You will have a window of 30 minutes before the conference call with Mr. Lee, the interior decorator at 5 o'clock.

⊃ 這例句的 window 並非是一般「窗戶」的意思。在這裡指的是一個窗口、一段空檔的意思。例：You will have <u>a window of</u> 20 minutes to talk to him before he leaves for the airport.（在他出發去機場前，你還有一個 20 分鐘的空檔可以逮到機會跟他講幾句話。）

Conference call 指電話連線會議。Conference call 在一般的跨國公司，或是進出口貿易等行業，都是很常見的會議模式；也是與國外廠商聯繫，或是跟分公司開會很常見的溝通模式。有時候甚至是三方以上的通話（three-way conference call），方便分公司與總公司可以快速地召開簡潔有力的會議，以佈達訊息或是討論與大家相關的議題。

秘書特助經驗分享

　　助理工作需要當機立斷，你會遇上各種突發狀況。冷靜地應對問題、靈活地調度工作內容讓 day to day operation（日常運作）正常進行，就是特助最基本的必備條件。除了頭腦要動得快之外，文書處理方面（organizing and maintaining files on a daily basis）你也需要高人一等。每天組織和歸檔各種文件，讓上司更方便讀取，或是日後找資料更迅速，也是特助少不了的工作項目之一。你是否也具備這些需要細心與耐心的工作能力呢？

❶ 秘書特助篇

❷ 秘書特助行銷公關篇

MEMO

UNIT 8

活動出席確認或婉拒

Confirming or declining attending an event

 秘書特助工作內容介紹

作為一個特助，除了有時候要代替主管出席活動之外，還需要懂得委婉地說「不」！The art of saying no is crucial. 如何禮貌地拒絕邀約，是一門學問。這點在時尚產業尤其重要；數不清的酒會、記者會、新品發表會、媒體公關活動與頒獎典禮，與自己屬性不太相同或是撞期的時候，你會有機會婉拒出席。你絕對不能臨時缺席，以免成為廠商的拒絕往來戶。你可以親自跑一趟或是透過電話表達歉意，只要不要透過 FB 或簡訊，多一點人性的互動，就可以降低拒絕的殺傷力。

職場上實況對談的一問二答　 Track 08

① 秘書特助篇

② 秘書特助行銷公關篇

有些人很難將「不」說出口，深怕拒絕會傷害對方的感受。但適當的拒絕，對雙方絕對是利大於弊的。如果勉強參與與公司業務相距甚遠的活動，不但妨礙心情，之後依然得拒絕對方。以下是特助 Amilia、Ms. Kylie 和公關 Oliver 的問答：

Question 1

K **Amilia, I got 5 tickets to the sports equipment expo from a bicycle company. They are inviting me to test ride their new products. Not knowing how to ride a bicycle totally makes me feel uncomfortable. And I will not enjoy being photographed in sportswear. Would you like to go instead or decline their invitation?**

愛蜜莉亞，我從自行車公司收到 5 張體育器材博覽的門票。他們邀請我去試乘新產品，但我會很不自在，因為我根本不會騎自行車，而且我也不喜歡穿運動服拍照。妳願意代替我去，或是婉拒他們的邀請嗎？

Possible answer 1

A That's an idea! Or we can give the tickets to the Sales Department. They go on a bike tour every weekend. I think they will enjoy the sports equipment expo so much more than we would. I will call PR and thank her for the tickets.

這是個辦法，或者我們可以把門票給業務部。他們每週末都安排騎車之旅。他們會比我們更樂於參與體育器材博覽會。我會打電話給公關，謝謝她的票。

Possible answer 2

Ⓐ Say no more, I don't mind going for you. I will personally be there to show our appreciation and thank them generously.

請交給我。我會親自表達我們的讚賞和感謝。

Question 2

Ⓞ Hi, Amilia. This is Oliver from Picture Perfect Magazine. I have sent you an e-mail about an interview with Ms. Kylie. We are looking for stories about career women who surely know how to strike a balance between life and work at the same time. Do you think you can schedule a meeting so that I can interview her? We can also have an telephone interview.

嗨，愛蜜莉亞，我是《完美生活雜誌》的奧利弗。我有發過電子郵件給妳，我們在尋找可以同時兼顧生活和工作的職業婦女，所以我們想採訪關於凱莉女士的故事。可以請妳幫我安排採訪的會面時間嗎？透過電話採訪也是可以的。

Possible answer 1

Ⓐ Hi, Oliver. Yes, I have gotten the e-mail and thank

you for the opportunity. As appealing as it is, I am sorry to inform you that Ms. Kylie won't be available for an interview for at least 2 months. She is currently working on a book and she will not accept any interviews until it's published. Please ask us again after if there are other suitable subjects for her.

你好，奧利弗，是的，我有收到您的電子郵件，感謝您給我們這個機會。雖然很吸引人，但很不巧的，凱莉小姐目前正忙著寫書，直到書籍上市之前，她這 2 個月是不接受採訪的。之後如果有適合我們的題材，請不吝與我們聯絡。

Possible answer 2

🅐 Thank you so much for keeping us in mind. However, I'm sorry we won't be able to help you this time. A dear friend of Ms. Kylie, who is a very successful career woman who works in real estate, might just be the ideal candidate. If you would consider it, I will pass on her contact information.

非常感謝您把我們放在心裡。我很抱歉，這次我們可能無法配合。不過凱莉小姐想推薦另外一個非常成功的職業婦女，她活躍於房地產業，也許是個很理想的人選。如果你願意考慮的話，我可以提供她的聯絡方式給您。

特助補給單字

expo *n.* 博覽會

decline *v.* 拒絕

 秘書特助對答技巧提點

I have gotten the e-mail and thank you for the opportunity. As appealing as it is, I am sorry to inform you that Ms. Kylie won't be available for an interview for at least 2 months. She is currently working on a book and she will not accept any interviews until it's published. Please ask us again after if there are other suitable subjects for her.

◎ 禮貌地拒絕約會，有幾個重點：首先，因為對方詢問是否有收到信，請先回答問題。記得在拒絕之前要先表達感謝，再誠心道歉。愛蜜莉亞先點出因為凱莉小姐手上有了先前安排的工作，所以無法配合採訪，並不是因為對於對方的邀約不感到興趣。最後，針對未來的合作預留空間，這樣禮貌地拒絕，會讓對方覺得受到尊重。

◎ 向對方表達感謝的其他說法：

Thank you for the enthusiasm and support.（謝謝你的熱情和支持。）

⊃ 預留未來合作空間的其他說法：

Please <u>keep us in mind for</u> future cooperation. （日後如果有合作機會，請記得我們。）

 秘書特助經驗分享

　　之前有提到婉拒邀約一定要本人親自處理，或是透過電話交代，才能讓拒絕帶有溫度，同時表達感謝。不過現在有很多邀約是透過網路平台發出訊息（稱做 online invitations），其中很多甚至是要你直接回覆：出席、可能出席，或是不出席。這樣的模式就可以直接回答參加或不參加，不需要再拜訪或是打電話，也不會顯得失禮。

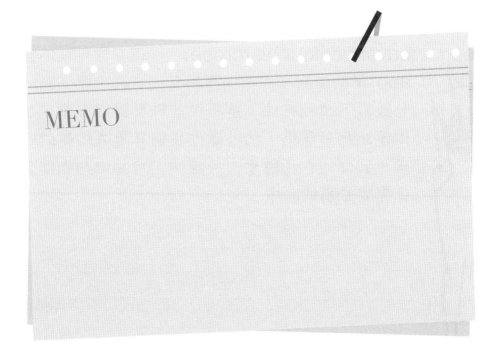

MEMO

UNIT 9 作老闆的門面
Representing your manager

 ## 秘書特助工作內容介紹

　　特助時常需要代替老闆出席聚會、替老闆擋駕或是接待客戶……等，因此適當的專業打扮是不可或缺的。一般來說淡妝、整齊乾淨與精緻的打扮更能替自己妝點出更專業的形象。擁有自己專屬的時尚範本，能讓你更有效運用你所有的衣物（Keeping a stylebook to help you advance your wardrobe.）。現在你可以下載 app 幫助你列出你衣櫥裡所有的衣褲、裙、鞋、包跟數不清的配件，這不但能夠幫助你分類，替你建議每日穿搭，也能讓你在週年慶失心瘋的時候，對你的衣物總量一目瞭然，冷靜地判斷你真正需要添購的品項！

職場上實況對談的一問二答

Track 09

❶ 秘書特助篇

❷ 秘書特助行銷公關篇

光鮮亮麗的時尚業，其實背後有著追著流行腳步，衣櫃永遠少一件的心酸。這時候不妨透過衣櫃的大掃除，仔細檢視自己的購買喜好。建議你找到適合自己風格的服飾店，與店家建立起良好的關係，如果有適合你的衣服，你就可以搶先看囉！以下是特助 Amilia 與精品服飾店店員 Boutique's clerk 的問答：

Question 1

🅱 **Hi, Amilia. We have fabulous linen button-downs and pencil skirts shipped in yesterday. When I saw them, I immediately thought of you. Do you have time to come in tomorrow and take a look? I will give you a 30% discount to thank you for introducing new customers to us.**

妳好，愛蜜莉亞，我們昨天店裡進了漂亮的亞麻排扣襯衫還有合身窄裙。我一看到它們，就馬上想到妳。妳明天有時間過來看看嗎？為了要謝謝妳幫介紹新客人，我這次會給你打七折喔！

Possible answer 1

🅐 I will swing by tomorrow after breakfast. I've been looking for a white button-down to go with the rest of my wardrobe and I wouldn't mind adding a pencil skirt into my work outfits. With a few accessories, I think they make any shirts look tidy and professional.

我明天吃完早餐後會過去一趟。我最近一直在找白色襯衫，好搭配我其他的衣服。也許買件合身窄裙也不錯，讓我的上班服加點變化。只要稍加一點飾品，它會讓簡單的上衣看起來正式又有型。

Possible answer 2

Ⓐ I am quite busy this month; I don't think I will have any time in the next two weeks. But the linen button-down sounds appealing; do you think you can deliver them to my office so that I can try them on?

我這個月挺忙的，我接下來的 2 週可能都抽不出空來。但亞麻襯衫很吸引我，你可以把它們送到我的辦公室，好讓我試穿一下嗎？

Question 2

Ⓑ Hi, Amilia. This is Jenny from the boutique. The vine green motor jacket in nubuck that you have ordered has arrived. All the details including its cropped design with hip pockets and the fold over collar, are delicately made. I can't wait to check them out with you! Would you like to come over and try them on to see if they fit?

妳好，愛蜜莉亞，我是精品店的珍妮，妳訂購的藤綠色磨砂牛皮騎士夾克已經到貨囉！短版剪裁、翻折領口和口袋設

計，所有的細節都作工精細。我等不及要和妳一起看新品
了！妳想過來試試看是否合身嗎？

Possible answer 1

Ⓐ Great news. I was wondering when they would arrive. Tell you what. I will go try them on during my lunch hour today. If any of them fits perfectly, I will place an order for the black one.

真是好消息，我正在想它什麼時候會到呢！告訴你吧，我今
天的午飯時間會過去試穿，如果很適合的話，我要直接買一
件黑色的。

Possible answer 2

Ⓐ Good. I will try to make it tomorrow. In addition, I need a red dress to attend a book release next weekend; do you think you could also lay out a few red dresses for me so I can try them on as well?

好的，我會盡量明天找時間過去。此外，我需要一件紅色禮
服出席下週末的新書發表會，妳可以幫我挑幾件紅色禮服，
好讓我一起試穿嗎？

特助補給單字

linen *n.* 亞麻

button-down *n.* 排扣襯衫

pencil skirt *n.* 直筒長裙

秘書特助對答技巧提點

I will give you a 30% discount to thank you for introducing new customers to us.

➲ 折扣的概念我們的習慣是乘以折扣數，比方說 4 折就是總價乘以 0.4 的意思。但美式的算法則是以去掉百分比數的方式來思考，如果是以 4 折來說，就會是 60 percent off，總價少掉百分之六十的意思。所以 10 percent off = 9 折，20 percent off = 8 折，以此類推。例：I got a 40 percent off coupon from my last purchase.（我上次消費拿到了一張六折的折價卷。）

I've been looking for a white button-down to go with the rest of my wardrobe and I wouldn't mind adding a pencil skirt into my work outfits.

➲ wardrobe 簡單來說是衣櫃的意思，但它更貼切的含義是泛指你所有的衣物、配件甚是是鞋子。因此 wardrobe 是很可以看出你個人喜好與特質的方式。

to go with something 這個片語的意思是與某個事、物作搭配。例如：I still need a knit hat to go with my winter outfits. Then my wardrobe can be considered complete for now.（我還需要一頂針織帽來搭配我的冬裝，那這樣我的衣物就算暫時完整了。）

秘書特助經驗分享

不知道當一個時尚助理該如何穿搭嗎？多看一些國外影集吧！就算是韓劇，也有很多圍繞著辦公室話題而衍生的戲劇，其中的穿搭與妝髮都是你可以學習的。剛開始學習打扮得體，有幾個大原則，第一、避免濃妝、第二、避免太過裸露、第三、全身的顏色不要超過三個、第四、注重整潔、第五、避免穿牛仔褲，最後，高跟鞋不要穿太高，你會有很多跑腿的機會。

❶ 秘書特助篇

❷ 秘書特助行銷公關篇

MEMO

替老闆跑腿
Running errands

 ## 秘書特助工作內容介紹

　　時尚產業的助理角色，除了公事需要負責，經常也要一併處理老闆的私事。小至買咖啡、領送洗的禮服、接送小孩、代為選購長輩的禮物、甚至是跑公家機關辦理證件等雜事。其實作為一個助理，做這些跑腿工作是很正常的。為了不延宕日常的工作，你必須懂得如何安排時間、做事有條有理，並擁有絕佳的記性。然而最重要的還是要瞭解主管的喜好。代為處理事情的方式，不能以自己的出發點，而是要以主管的視角，以更貼心細緻的手法，讓事情更加圓滿。

職場上實況對談的一問二答

Track 10

助理要在緊縮的時間裡處理突發狀況,長時間的打電話協調與跑不完的小行程(run errands),這就是時尚業助理的小縮影。但經過這樣的千錘百鍊,你會一次比一次駕輕就手。以下是 Amilia 與醫院 Hospital: H 和精品店店員 Faith (Boutique clerk): F 之間的問答:

Question 1

🄷 Taipei General Hospital Dental Department. How may I help you today?

台北總醫院牙科部,有什麼能幫助您的嗎?

Possible answer 1

🄰 Hello, this is Amilia Huang calling for Ms. Lillian Kylie. She has terrible pain in one of her wisdom teeth, and would like to schedule an emergency dental appointment.

您好,我是愛蜜莉亞・黃,代替莉莉恩・凱莉小姐撥電話過來。她有一顆智齒發痛,緊急需要看牙科。

Possible answer 2

🄰 Hello, this is Amilia Huang from Ms. Kylie's office. I am calling on behalf of Lillian Kylie to reschedule her teeth cleaning on November 2nd at 6 PM..

您好，我是凱莉小姐辦公室的助理愛蜜莉亞·黃。我代替莉莉恩·凱莉小姐打電話過來更改她 11 月 2 日的下午 6 點的洗牙門診。

Question 2

F Hello, Amilia. How are you? Welcome to our boutique. What can I do for you today?

艾蜜莉亞您好，歡迎光臨。今天能為您提供什麼服務呢？

Possible answer 1

A Hi, Faith. I am fine, thank you. I am here to shop for my boss' 80-year-old grandmother's birthday gift. I am totally swamped with work and have no gift ideas, so I thought maybe you could help me out.

你好，菲思。我很好，謝謝。我今天來是要幫我老闆採購她 80 歲祖母的生日禮物。我最近工作忙得焦頭爛額，對於買什麼禮物，完全沒有頭緒，所以我想也許你可以幫助我。

Possible answer 2

A Hello, Faith. I am terrific. Thank you for asking. I am here to buy a gift for my boss to give it to her daughter. She just turned 11 and loves music. She will probably enjoy a piece of unique musical equipment.

您好，菲思，我非常好，謝謝妳的關心。我是來買禮物送給我老闆的女兒。她剛滿 11 歲和十分熱愛音樂。她應該會很喜歡特殊的樂器。

> 特助補給單字

dental *adj.* 牙科的

terrific *adj.* 好極了

unique *adj.* 特殊的

秘書特助對答技巧提點

I am calling on behalf of Lillian Kylie to reschedule her teeth cleaning on November 2nd 6 PM.

- Reschedule 重新預約。Re+原型動詞通常是「重複」後面那個動詞的意思。比方說 re+apply=reapply 重新申請也是這樣的用法。例：My flight was cancelled due to the weather condition, so I have to reschedule our appointment.（我的班機因為天氣不佳所以被取消了，所以我得重新安排會議的時間。）

I am here to shop for my boss' 80 years old grandmother's birthday gift. I am totally swamped with work and have no gift ideas, so I thought maybe you could help me out.

- Swamp 的名詞是沼澤的意思，當成動詞來用有陷入泥濘、陷入困境或是忙不過來意思。例：Being an executive assistant is a hard job with countless tasks to be done in such little time; however, it hasn't swamped me yet. （作為一個行政助理並不容易，在每天有限的時間內都有無數的任務必須完成，但它並沒有打敗我呢！）

秘書特助經驗分享

　　擔心會漏掉主管的代辦事項嗎？請隨身帶著筆記本和筆，並且隨手備份在手機裡。如果怕寫得慢，請先用語音記事本，把代辦事項錄下來，回到座位上後再按照優先順序去排行程。你一定得準備有日期的行事曆，最好是一天有一整頁可以寫備忘錄的形式，這樣才可以一目瞭然你一整個禮拜、一整個月，甚至這一整季有哪些事情得先計劃安排。

MEMO

和廠商交涉

Negotiating with vendors and suppliers

 秘書特助工作內容介紹

　　時尚產業的助理工作，之所以令人夢寐以求，是因為在替主管處理代辦事項的時候，可以接觸各樣的廠商。與廠商溝通的過程當中，你會學到可貴的產業知識，這些都是學校學不到的喔！與製造商和供應商直接接觸，是瞭解時尚產業最快的方式（Interacting with suppliers and vendors will get you familiar with the fashion industry in no time.）。時尚產業追隨著全世界的潮流走，因此你得學會耳聽八方與快速應變，才不會被這個產業所淘汰。

職場上實況對談的一問二答 Track 11

時尚產業所包含的品項繁多，比方說彩妝、時裝與時尚配件等，因此相關的上下游製造廠商，與供應商更是不勝枚舉。以下是助理 Amilia 與廠商 Vendors 交涉可能出現的問題：

Question 1

Ⓥ Hey, Amilia. I have gotten your request for the petal soft cashmere scarf. As for now the factory has got 3 petal shades for you to choose from, and I have sent the samples to you 2 days ago. If you have received them, would you please confirm the color with me today?

嗨，愛蜜莉亞，我有收到你想要粉色喀什米爾圍巾的需求。目前工廠現有 3 種粉色調可供選擇。2 天前我已經寄出樣品給您了。如果您有收到的話，今天方便幫我確認顏色嗎？

Possible answer 1

Ⓐ Thank you so much for the fast delivery. Yes. I have received the samples. However we are looking for more of the color of cherry blossom, instead of fuchsia pink. The sample colors are not going to match the shade of pink that we are looking for.

謝謝您這麼有效率，是的，我已經收到樣品了。但是我們要的粉色系是比較偏向櫻花的顏色，而不是紫紅色。您寄來的樣品，有點偏離我們想要的粉色形象。

Possible answer 2

🅐 Yes, of course. Among the 3 samples that you have sent us, we absolutely loved the salmon pink scarf. Nevertheless, do you think you can lighten up the fabric? We are actually looking for something that's more translucent, would that be a possibility?

當然沒問題。在您送來的 3 個樣品之中,我們非常喜歡那橘紅色圍巾,但是布料方面是否能再輕巧一點?我們其實更想要有點半透明的材質,這方面有可行性嗎?

Question 2

🅐 **We are planning to launch another fedora hat this winter since our last design was such a hit. This time we are going for a vintage look. Maybe we can over some materials for that look?**

有鑑於上一個設計的成功銷售,我們正計劃在今年冬天推出另一款軟呢帽。這次我們想要尋求復古風,可以針對這樣的元素給我們看一些樣品嗎?

Possible answer 1

🅥 Very well, first of all, we can go for a darker color such as burgundy or emerald. Secondly, wool would be a good choice because it's a perfect texture, and affordable at the same time.

很好，首先我們可以選深色系，像是酒紅色或是墨綠色。其次，羊毛是一個不錯的選擇，因為它的質感完美，同時價格實惠。

Possible answer 2

🅥 Yes, you may and you are in luck. We just got new materials last week and they might just be what you are looking for. The wide brim fedora would look sensational in this charcoal felted wool.

當然可以，而且妳來得正是時候。我們上週才進了新材料，它可能正是你要找的合適材質。寬邊圓頂軟呢帽如果用這塊黑炭色羊毛氈來製作，視覺效果會非常好。

特助補給單字

shade *n.* 濃淡、色度

blossom *n.* 開花

lighten *v.* 減輕

translucent *adj.* 半透明的

hit *n.* 成功、蔚為風潮

vintage *n.* 復古

brim *n.* 帽緣

fedora *n.* 軟呢帽

秘書特助對答技巧提點

Among the 3 samples that you have sent us, we absolutely loved the salmon pink scarf. Nevertheless, do you think you can lighten up the fabric? We are actually looking for something that's more translucent, would that be a possibility?

➲ 文中愛蜜莉亞提到他們非常喜歡寄過來的樣品，但希望在材質上做調整。在跟廠商對話當中，如果十分確定樣品值得採購，然而仍有需要修正的地方，這時候請別忘記先說點稱讚的話，再提出你的要求。例：We really like the color combination and the fitting is so flattering. We are really looking forward to the new design. On the other hand, do you think we can minimize the beading details since our target audience are in their 20s? （我們真的很喜歡這次的顏色搭配和修飾身形的剪裁，大家都非常期待新品的設計；另一方面，你覺得我們可以盡量減少珍珠飾品的部分嗎？因為我們的目標客戶定位在 20 世代。）

秘書特助經驗分享

　　與廠商交涉前請先記得做功課，如果你是新手，不懂的地方可以向前輩請教，並且多涉獵行內的專業名詞。如果你所負責的產業是皮包飾品類，你知道 shopper bags 與 tote bags 之間的差別嗎？購物袋與托特包，主要的差別在於功能性與材質。購物袋通常是方形的帆布材質包。而托特包通常是雙把手，並有開放式的隔層處理。（A shopper bag is usually rectangular in shape, often in canvas materials. On the other hand, a tote bag is usually double handled with an open compartment.）時尚業世界如此寬廣，學問可多得很呢！

MEMO

對於所有部門動向瞭若指掌

Monitoring trends in all business sectors

 ### 秘書特助工作內容介紹

　　公司組織裡可能有行銷部、業務部、門市部、財務部、管理部、人事部等，大家各司其職，有重大決議時會由某部門召開會議，由大家各派代表出席。而特助經常需要代替主管參加會議，無論是佈達訊息或去作會議記錄，目的是讓主管在百忙之中仍然可以熟悉各部門的營運動態。平日特助也要多與別部門的同事有交流，中午一起吃飯或下班後聚餐，以建立互相的信賴與友善。在做自己部門的決策時，也能更設身處地為其他人著想，讓公司的運作更流暢。

職場上實況對談的一問二答　 Track 12

通常部門的月會大家都會出席，重要的訊息頒佈也會在月會進行，所以特助最好都能夠列席，以確保不漏掉任何消息。月會也是認識公司同仁與聯絡感情的好機會，也會有機會碰到高階主管，或是外派的同事等等。以下是 Amilia 與 Ms. Kylie 針對其他部門的問答：

Question 1

Ⓚ Amilia! A minute please! From your meeting minutes, there are a few topics between the Marketing and Sales Departments that don't seem to go eye to eye. Is that going to affect our product purchasing in the fall?

愛蜜莉亞，請過來一下！妳的會議記錄上提到，行銷部和業務部，似乎有些事情無法達成共識，這會影響到我們的秋季的採購嗎？

Possible answer 1

Ⓐ Well, the Sales Department's concern is mainly about the inventory from the last season; however, Marketing is working on a new product's marketing campaign, which caused a bit of a conflict at the meeting.

業務部門主要是對上一季的庫存有疑慮，但行銷部目前還是積極地規劃新品的行銷活動，所以在會議上起了一點衝突。

77

Possible answer 2

🅐 Our purchasing plan will go accordingly, though they did mention that they have doubts about the low-rise trousers and English sleeves. Perhaps we can share some fashion week fashion tips about how to accessorize and how they would work on different body types.

我們的採購計劃不會改變,雖然他們有提到,對低腰褲和英式蓬袖有點疑慮。或許我們可以分享來自時裝週的穿搭技巧或是如何使用配件,好讓不同身型的顧客都找出適合穿著的方式。

Question 2

🅚 Thank you for coming in, George. The secretary will walk you out. Please contact Human Resources if you have any other questions. Amilia, did you want to talk to me?

感謝你過來一趟,喬治,秘書會送你出去。如果你有任何問題,請聯繫人力資源部。愛蜜莉亞,你剛才找我嗎?

Possible answer 1

🅐 Yes, Ms. Kylie. Human Resources has informed me that since social media such as Twitter, Facebook and Instagram are so widely used in the fashion industry, there are few guidelines that our company wishes all of us to follow.

是的，凱莉小姐，人力資源有告知我因為社群媒體的發達，如 Tweeter、Facebook 和 Instagram 在時尚業的風行，公司希望我們都能遵守一些規則。

Possible answer 2

🅐 Yes, Ms. Kylie. As social networks bloom in the fashion industry, Human Resources has sent out a memo to all the departments about social media guidelines. The first guideline is to think before you post. HR also encourages us to start a conversation on social media, that will keep followers coming back.

是的，凱莉小姐，因為社交網絡在時尚界的發光發亮，人力資源發出了一份備忘錄到公司所有的部門，希望大家遵守幾個大原則。第一個規定是，請充分思考後再發文。HR 也鼓勵大家在社交媒體促進對話，這樣可以吸引關注者再回來。

特助補給單字

guideline *n.* 規定

bloom *v.* 蓬勃發展

秘書特助篇 ❶

秘書特助行銷公關篇 ❷

秘書特助對答技巧提點

From your meeting minutes, there are a few topics between the Marketing and Sales Departments that don't seem to go eye to eye. Is that going to affect our product purchasing in the fall?

⊃ Go eye to eye 是同意、達成共識的意思。另有常見用法 see eye to eye。例 1：My boss and I usually go eye to eye except lunch preferences.（我老闆和我通常很有共識，唯獨午飯的偏好相差甚遠。）例 2：It's difficult for Marketing and Sales Department to see eye to eye. That's when upper management comes in and make a decision.（行銷部和業務部通常很難達成協議，這時候就需要高層介入，並作出最後的決定。）

As social networks bloom in the fashion industry, Human Resources has sent out a memo to all the departments about social media guidelines.

⊃ Bloom 原意是花滿開的意思，也常被用來當成蓬勃發展與繁榮的意思。例 1：Roses bloom throughout the years, so it's a very desirable garden flower.（玫瑰因為一年四季都可以開花，所以是很受歡迎的花園植物。）例 2：Real estate was blooming for the past 10 years until now.（房地產過去 10 年持續的蓬勃發展，直到現在才停滯。）

秘書特助經驗分享

　　完全掌握各部門的動態，還有一個訣竅，就是你得尊重對方的專業。很多時候開會起衝突，都是因為認為自己的意見才正確而發生。但市場是開放的，也有各種不同的消費族群，懂得接納不一樣的聲音，對你的工作態度也會有幫助。跟你不同部門的同事，擁有的專業一定不一樣，多以請教的方式，虛心學習，對方也會對你釋出善意的。

MEMO

UNIT 13 跨部門工作支援

Inter-departmental support

秘書特助工作內容介紹

　　特助除了協助主管的工作，也常需要代替主管參與會議，以及作為主管和其他部門的溝通橋梁。公司舉辦活動或是臨時動議，助理都得在第一時間提醒上司，作應有的配合與行動。有時候特助也得扮演著支援者的角色，以補足公司不足的人力或技能。助理的可塑性一定要強，而且得願意在危機出現的時候挺身而出。這樣主管絕對會越來越信賴你，將更重要的事情交給你處理。當你願意為團隊付出，上司與同事也會願意帶領你，你在時尚界的路就會越寬廣。

職場上實況對談的一問二答

 Track 13

公司別的部門如果開口要求支援，你應該要好好把握這個機會。助理多跟其他部門有來往，絕對會有利於你的工作。事實上公司的每個部門都是相輔相成的，彼此之間一定會有競爭關係，而公司辦活動的時候，就是很好的修補時機。以下是特助 Amilia 與行銷部門 Marketing: Ryder 和 Ms. Kylie 之間的問答：

Question 1

Ｒ Hi, Amilia. According to our last meeting, the pop-up store in shin yi district will need the Fashion Department to assist with the window display and prop decorations. We are one person short in the product introduction team; do you think you can fill in on that day?

嗨，愛蜜莉亞，根據我們上一次的會議決議，信義區快閃店我們將會需要精品部協助窗口陳列和店內裝飾。另外我們產品介紹組還少一個人，你那天可以幫忙嗎？

Possible answer 1

Ａ Hi, Ryder. Thanks for the reminder. We are finalizing the design of the props right now. After tomorrow's meeting, we will confirm the design and send it out to be constructed. As for the product introduction, as long as you provide the sales kit 2 days prior to the store opening, I will be happy to

83

give you a hand.

萊德您好，感謝您的提醒。現在我們即將要完成道具的設計，明天的會議後，我們會確認最終版的設計並發派製作。至於產品的介紹，只要您在開店 2 天前提供銷售資料給我，我會很樂意幫忙的。

Possible answer 2

Ⓐ Hello, Ryder. We are purchasing the accessories and ordering fresh flowers for the store opening. We are very pleased with the decorating progress. As for the product introduction, I am afraid I can't stay more than 2 hours. However, I will arrange for one of our team members to fill in for the position. Would that be all right?

萊德您好，我們正在購買飾品和訂購鮮花來佈置快閃店，我們很滿意目前裝飾陳列的進度。至於產品的介紹，我那天恐怕沒辦法待超過 2 小時。不過我可以安排我們的團隊成員之一來填補那個位置，這樣的安排可以嗎？

Question 2

Ⓚ Amilia, could you come in for a minute? I am sending you out to train one of our new distributors in the east district. Our next product training is not scheduled for another month, so I am going to need you to assist them. You think

you can be ready in 2 days?

愛蜜莉亞，妳可以進來一下嗎？我要派你去教育訓練東區一家新的經銷商。我們下一次的產品訓練還要一個月，所以我需要妳來幫助他們。妳可以在 2 天內準備好嗎？

Possible answer 1

🅐 Yes, Ms. Kylie. I am very familiar with all of our luxury items, from brand value, designers, materials to design concepts. I will be able to help them with any product knowledge.

好的，凱莉小姐，我對我們所有的產品都很熟悉，從品牌價值、設計師、材質和設計理念都難不倒我。任何產品的相關知識我都給他們解答。

Possible answer 2

🅐 Yes, 2-day preparation is perfect. First, I will confirm their inventory, prepare the product sheets, and run them by you. Secondly, I will contact them to book a suitable time for the product training. Finally, I will arrange everything in advance, so while I am not in the office, the office won't be unattended.

是的，2 天剛剛好。首先我會先確認他們的進貨狀況、準備適合他們的產品表，並交給您過目。其次，我會與他們聯繫，預約產品訓練合適的時間。最後，我將提前做安排，所以當我不在辦公室的時候，公事都還是可以正常運行。

📋 特助補給單字

construct *v.* 建構

unattended *adj.* 無人看守的

 秘書特助對答技巧提點

First, I will confirm their inventory, prepare the product sheets, and run them by you. Secondly, I will contact them to book a suitable time for the product training. Finally, I will arrange everything in advance, so while I am not in the office, the office won't be unattended.

➲ First, secondly, finally... 第一點、第二點、最後，這樣的陳述方式，可以讓聽者輕易地分辨出重點在哪裡。逐項地解釋你接下來的做法，也很適合必須要時時刻刻知道進度的主管；清楚地解答他的問題，他就能放心地交給你處理，以避免他每十五分鐘就問你一次喔！這樣的表達方式也很常見於說明書或是食譜上。例：First, preheat the oven to 300 degrees. Secondly, stir flour, baking soda salt and chocolate powder in a large mixing bowl. Finally, line up 10 muffin cups and pour the mixture into them and put in oven for baking.（首先，烤箱預熱至 300 度，其次，在大碗中攪拌麵粉、小蘇打、鹽和巧克力粉。最後，排好 10 個鬆餅杯，將混合物倒進去，並放進烤箱烘烤。）

We are one person short in the product introduction team; do you think you can fill in on that day?

⊃ Short 短少，缺少。常用的方式也有 be short of ...，例：We <u>are short of</u> staff this week. Could you help out in the store for at least 2 days?（我們這週很缺人手，你可以起碼過來幫忙 2 天嗎？）

 ## 秘書特助經驗分享

　　跨部門的聯絡窗口，常常是落在助理身上，因此你一定要用心聽別人的需求，並且用對方聽得懂的方式跟他溝通。如果是跟業務部討論，你可以多用銷售術語和促進業績的成長的方向來要求對方配合。這樣不但能有效率達到目標，也能夠同時減少部門之間的摩擦。

MEMO

辦公室用品管理與預算控制

Office supplies management and budget control

 秘書特助工作內容介紹

　　助理工作的庶務之一，包含了辦公室的管理。文件的分類、歸檔、硬體與軟體的規劃、採購與存放，雖然看起來不起眼，卻能夠維持公司的行政效率與專業性。時尚界的行政助理需要維持一定的辦公用品庫存以及預算控制和採購（Fashion industry executive assistant needs to maintain office supply inventory, as well as budget control and sourcing.）。為了維持最佳品質，同時為公司節省經費，尋找多個專業廠商與比價也是不可或缺的工作喔！身為時尚助理的你，每一分一毫的努力，再加上大家各盡其職，都幫助成就了時尚界絢麗的成果。

職場上實況對談的一問二答　　Track 14

時尚界的資料庫與樣品多到數不清，所以良好的資料庫整理能讓公司有效地運作。我們可以透過問答的方式來瞭解，好的倉庫管理系統該有哪些條件。以下是特助 Amilia 與廠商 Vendor 之間的問答：

Question 1

🅥 **Hi, Amilia. I am calling to see if you have received our fax about the critical elements for our inventory system. I want to make sure that our program will cover all your needs and concerns.**

嗨，愛蜜莉亞，我打電話給您是要跟您確認是否有收到我們的傳真，內容是關於庫存系統不可缺少的關鍵要素。希望我們的設計能涵蓋您所有的需求。

Possible answer 1

🅐 Thank you for calling sir. I am looking at it as we speak. I can see that location labels are extremely important. Not only does it have to be easy to read and straightforward, it also has to be well-organized.

先生，謝謝您的來電。我們說話的同時，我正在看傳真呢！我可以看得出來，位置的標示很重要，不僅要清楚易懂，還需要有組織性。

Possible answer 2

🅰 Hello, I was expecting your call. I haven't got the fax yet. Do you think you could fax it to me again? Also, I would like to make sure that it comes with the software that tracks all inventory activities since we have a lot of samples going in and out of the company daily.

您好，我正在等你的電話。我還沒有收到傳真呢，您可以再傳一次給我嗎？另外，我想確認傳真的內容有包含可以追蹤庫存的軟體，因為我們每天都有很多進出公司的樣品。

Question 2

🆅 **Hi, Amilia, I got your inquiry about the printing paper and 30 storage boxes. I was wondering if you have any preferences on the colors? We are low in stock of certain colors.**

嗨，愛蜜莉亞，我收到了妳的影印紙和 30 個儲物盒的訂單。我想知道妳對於儲物盒是否有顏色的喜好？我們某些顏色正處於低庫存。

Possible answer 1

🅰 Hello, I am glad you asked. Ms. Kylie only uses black storage boxes in her office, so please place more orders if you don't have enough in stock.

您好，我很高興你問了這個問題。凱莉小姐的辦公室只用黑色的儲物盒，所以如果您庫存不足的話，請再下訂單。

Possible answer 2

Ⓐ Hello, thank you for asking. We only use black and white storage boxes in our office. There is one other thing; can you give us a quotation for the acrylic magazine storage bins? I am looking for different sources for this item since we buy them pretty often.

您好，感謝您的詢問，我們的辦公室只使用黑色和白色的儲物箱。還有一件事，可以麻煩您給我壓克力雜誌儲物箱的報價嗎？我們很常採購這個物件，所以我想多找幾個廠商作比較。

■ 特助補給單字

inventory *n.* 庫存

acrylic *adj.* 壓克力的

storage bin *n.* 儲物箱

秘書特助對答技巧提點

I got your inquiry about the printing paper and 30 storage boxes./ Can you give us a quotation for the acrylic magazine storage bins?

➲ Inquiry 指訂單需求，詞性為名詞。Quotation 指報價，詞性也是名詞。 進行商品採購的時候，你會經常看到這兩個單字。假設你今天是下訂單的那一方，你會先發信給廠商，告知對方你的需求並且詢問報價。在發信的時候，e-mail 主旨記得放上「inquiry」這個字樣，信件才不會被忽略喔！以下我們以信件的方式，指導正確的報價詢問方式。

To: 收信方 e-mail
From: 自己的 e-mail
CC: 可以放相關人員的 e-mail，比方説 CC 給主管或同事。
Subject: Inquiry about 2016 new products 信件主旨：詢問新產品價格
Message: 信件內容
Hello Mr. Jacob,

This is Amilia Huang from Taiwan Boutique. Our shop locates in the center of Taipei. We carry products from numerous luxury brands and independent artists. We are very interested in your new collection in 2016. We are wondering if you can provide us the price list/quotation so that we can see if there is an opportunity of cooperation. Thanks in advance for your assistance.

您好，捷各布思先生，

我是台灣精品的愛蜜莉亞・黃。本店位於台北市中心，我們代理販售眾多精品品牌和獨立藝術家的產品。我們對於您 2016 年的全新系列很感興趣，不知您是否能提供給我們的價格表或是報價，好讓我們看看是否有合作的機會。先謝謝您撥冗處理。

❶ 秘書特助篇

❷ 秘書特助行銷公關篇

秘書特助經驗分享

文件或樣品管理請掌握好分類、減量與收納這三個原則。毀損和不會再使用的品項，請果斷地作報廢，公司有限的空間才能做最好的利用喔！在歸檔的時候，項目要簡潔有力，以名詞加形容詞來分類是最好的方式，比方說毛衣、紅色、XS 這樣的排序方式，會讓你快速地找到你要的東西。如果以形容詞或是尺寸作開頭，反而會增加時間成本！

UNIT 15 產品購買與庫存狀況
Product purchasing and monitoring inventories

 秘書特助工作內容介紹

　　當個稱職的時尚助理，會需要良好的英文能力。無論是與國外代理的品牌聯繫或是採購與詢價，都不能假手他人。而訂貨的後續處理與品牌經營層面，特助也需要瞭若指掌。有時候特助也會充當採購助理，負責建立訂單、貨品進度追蹤與庫存維護等問題（Sometimes executive assistant will also act as a purchasing assistant in order to create purchase orders, follow up and maintain inventory.）。產品的採購內容也許會由上司來決定，但下單前的相關問題處理、下單後的包裝運送與付款，會需要你的溝通技巧與良好的時間管理，才能圓滿達成喔！

職場上實況對談的一問二答 Track 15

台灣的時尚業很多都是爭取國外品牌的代理權，引進台灣後再依照市場需求，創造全新的品牌價值。如果是國際大品牌，也許在品牌精神與廣告方面的支援甚多，但操作空間相對比較受限。反之，年輕的品牌也許在經營上需要更費心，但在行銷與銷售端點就擁有較多彈性空間。以下是 Amilia 與首飾設計師品牌 Designer Accessories: Dee 之間的問答：

Question 1

D **Hello, Amilia. Thanks so much for reaching out! We have our own platform where you will be able to view our line sheets, including the name of the products, size and colors, item numbers, wholesale prices, and the recommended retail prices. There is a 10 thousand US dollar pre-paid balance, and everything you order can be deducted from the amount. Do you have any questions for now?**

您好愛蜜莉亞，非常感謝您的聯絡！我們擁有自己的訂購平台，可以看到我們的貨品資料，內容包括產品名稱、尺寸、顏色、商品編號、批發價和建議零售價。另外有一萬美元的預付款，您所訂購所有商品可以從預付金額中直接扣除。針對以上的內容是否有任何問題呢？

Possible answer 1

Ⓐ Hello, Dee. Thank you for the information. All the terms look pretty good. We are looking forward to working with you. We might not be able to pay upfront because it's against our company policy.

蒂兒妳好，謝謝您的解釋，所有條款都看起來沒什麼大問題。我們很期待能與您的合作。只是我們可能無法支付前期的預付款，因為它違反我們公司的規定。

Possible answer 2

Ⓐ Thank you so much for the detailed explanation. Our goal is to provide one of a kind accessories for our customers, so we would like to be your agent in Taiwan.

非常感謝妳的詳細解釋。我們的目標是提供客戶獨一無二的配件，因此我們想拿到台灣的代理權。

Question 2

Ⓟ **Amilia, how are you? I got your message about the items that have defects. According to the photos that you have shown me, I think the cause was due to the package. In future shipments, we will add more cushioning materials to prevent this problem from happening again. To compensate, would you**

like us to resend the products or credit you?

愛蜜莉亞，你好嗎？我收到關於產品缺陷的訊息了。根據你寄來的照片，我覺得原因是出於包裝。未來在裝運上我們將增加更多的緩衝材，以防止這個問題再度發生。為了彌補這個錯誤，請問你們希望我們重新寄送產品，或是退還成購物點數呢？

Possible answer 1

Ⓐ Hi, Dee. It's always good to hear from you! Thank you for taking action so soon. We would like to have the products replaced, please. Also, product item number 1191977 and 4151980 are both low in stock. We would like to place 500 pieces for each, so you may prepare them all in one shipment.

嗨蒂兒，總是很開心聽到妳的聲音！感謝您這麼快就採取行動。請幫我們寄產品來替換吧！此外，產品項目編號 1191977 和 4151980 的庫存都偏低了，我們想各下單 500 個，妳可以全部一起做運送。

Possible answer 2

Ⓐ Hi, Dee. I was just about to call you. About our pervious order, it was supposed to arrive last week, but I still haven't gotten it. Do you think you can check the shipping status for me?

嗨，蒂兒，我正要打電話給妳。關於我們上次的訂單，本來上週應該要送達的，但是目前還是沒有收到。你可以幫我檢查一下運送狀態嗎？

┃ *特助補給單字*

line sheet *ph.* 貨品資料

cushioning material *ph.* 緩衝材

compensate *v.* 彌補

 秘書特助對答技巧提點

We might not be able to pay upfront because it's against our company policy.

⊃ Against 違反。例 1：We don't usually have a sale during the year because it's <u>against</u> our brand policy. （我們通常年中是不會有打折的，因為這違反我們的品牌策略。）例 2：Please don't go <u>against</u> the traffic when you ride the bicycle.（騎腳踏車的時候請不要逆向。）

In future shipments, we will add more cushioning materials to prevent this problem from happening again. To compensate, would you like us to resend the products or credit you?

⊃ Compensate 彌補，這個動詞很常在貨品出瑕疵的時候出現。例 1：The shipment came with 2 broken packages, so some of the tops are not suitable for sale, can you <u>compensate</u> the loss by giving us store credits?（這批貨有兩個包裝損壞了，所以有一些上衣已經不適合銷售，你可以給我們購物點數以補償這些損失嗎？）例2：You can <u>compensate</u> your height by wearing Capri pants and heels.（你可以穿七分褲和高跟鞋來補強你身材嬌小的部分。）

 ## 秘書特助經驗分享

替公司採購的時候，很常會先代墊費用。開發票時務必請店家打上公司的統一編號，以利會計做帳。如果是車費或是其他無法開發票的公司行號，依然要記得拿收據，通常店家會蓋發票章，上面會有公司名稱與聯絡方式，回到公司後就能憑收據以開支請款單請款囉！

MEMO

UNIT 16 流行資訊搜集
Monitoring and collecting fashion trends

 秘書特助工作內容介紹

　　幫日理萬機的主管搜集產業訊息，如新產品、新材質、競爭者動向以及國外最新潮流等資訊，是特助經常性的工作（Monitoring fashion trends, competitors movement and updating your boss on the latest information might be one of assistants' daily tasks.）。各大時尚雜誌出刊的那一天，你就要全部整理好，標註好必看的內容。國外時尚網站有值得關注的 fashion news，就要第一時間把網頁連結寄給他。任何對老闆可能有幫助的訊息，你都要隨時提供給他。你不只是他的左右手，你甚至得當他的眼睛和耳朵。他需要什麼消息，你就要想辦法運用關係幫他找到。

職場上實況對談的一問二答

市場流行資訊調查對時尚業來說是家常便飯，如果你對時尚業有著高度熱誠，相信你的網路瀏覽前五名大概都是服飾品牌網站、時尚雜誌或是時尚部落格。你會不知不覺地想追蹤時尚的動態，為新出來的款式或是廣告而著迷，而這些市場動態都會對你的工作有幫助，也有助你的思考與銷售。以下是特助 Amilia 與老闆 Ms. Kylie 的問答：

Question 1

🅚 **Why are you so fascinated by "*The Blonde Salad*"? I see you visit this website almost every week.**

你為什麼對 *The Blonde Salad* 這麼著迷？我看妳幾乎每個星期都在看這個網站。

Possible answer 1

🅐 Run by Chiara Ferragni, *The Blonde Salad* is a fashion blog. The owner, Chiara Ferragni turned it into a multi-million dollar business. Now she has 14 staff to help her run the website and update fashion reports constantly. *The Blonde Salad* has evolved into a digital magazine that's separated from Chiara Ferragni's personal life.

The Blonde Salad 是時尚部落客琪亞拉·法拉格尼的網站，她已經把它經營成一個價值數百萬的企業。現在，她有

14 個員工，可以幫助她不斷地在網站上更新時尚訊息。 *The Blonde Salad* 已經演變成與琪亞拉·法拉格尼個人生活分開的網路雜誌。

Possible answer 2

Ⓐ Well, Chiara Ferragni is a very popular fashion blogger who established the blog called "*The Blonde Salad*". Her beauty and unique fashion have brought her fame and wealth; her successful business was even included as a case study in Harvard Business School for the MBA program.

是的，十分受歡迎的時尚部落客琪亞拉·法拉格尼成立了 *The blonde Salad* 網站。她的美麗和獨特的時尚風格不僅替她帶來了名氣和財富；她成功的企業甚至被列入哈佛商學院 MBA 課程的案例研究。

Question 2

Ⓚ **For the fashion shoots preparation, we are so close to being ready except for the shoes. Something just doesn't seem right. I need you to provide some other ideas for the shoes.**

這次的服裝拍攝我們幾乎都準備好了，就是鞋子我還是不太滿意。我需要妳提供些靈感給我。

Possible answer 1

Ⓐ Of course, I am more than happy to assist. From my

observations of all the major fashion media, I think pointy flats could be a good choice. Flats might seem casual, but with a pointy toe design, they will become formal and elegant. Pointy toe flats with the right material will have the same effects as high heels without sacrificing comfort.

當然，我很樂意。從我對各大時尚媒體的觀察看來，尖頭平底鞋應該是個不錯的選擇。平底鞋看起來太過輕鬆，但如果搭配上尖頭設計，就會變得正式而優雅。選對合適的材料能讓尖頭鞋和高跟鞋具有相同的修飾效果，卻不犧牲舒適性。

Possible answer 2

Ⓐ Yes, perhaps we can go for a brighter color, such as red or bright pink. They will not only pop in a photo, but also be seen on celebrities and a few other fashion icons.

好的，也許我們可以選擇更亮的顏色，例如大紅色或是搶眼的粉紅色。它們不僅在照片上搶眼，這一季也曾經出現在許多明星和時尚名媛的身上。

▌特助補給單字

digital *adj.* 數位

blogger *n.* 部落客

wealth *n.* 財富

observation *n.* 觀察

icon *n.* 偶像

 ## 秘書特助對答技巧提點

Now she has 14 staff to help her run the website and update fashion reports constantly.

➲ Run 在這裡的用法不是跑步而是經營的意思。一個企業需要很多人的協助，才能順利運行，因此這個「run」 就是透過某人或一群人的努力，讓這個機構能夠「運轉」的意思。例：Who runs the manufacture here?（誰是這個生產線的負責人？）

The Blonde Salad has evolved into a digital magazine that's separated from Chiara Ferragni's personal life.

➲ Evolve 是動詞「進化」的意思。這個句子的涵義是這個網站透過各種發展的演變，已經晉升為讓時尚界可作為指標與靈感的網路雜誌。另外一個常見的名詞 evolution，就是人類的「進化」。

例：Our relationship has evolved from best friends to families.（我們的關係從最好的朋友進化成家人了。）

From my observations of all the major fashion media, I think pointy flats could be a good choice.

◗ from my observation... 「從我的觀察看來……」 這句話請把它記下來。當老闆問你問題的時候，加上這句話可以讓對方認為，你平日就會自動自發去做市調與關心產業動向。所以突然被問問題的時候，也游刃有餘。例：From my observation, our one piece is making sale during weekdays. So if we do promotion on the dresses, we should probably avoid the weekends to maximize sales.（根據我的觀察，我們的連身洋裝平日賣得最好，所以如果要促銷洋裝，或許應該避開週末以求銷量最大化。）

 秘書特助經驗分享

網路世界與社群網站的發達，讓時尚界的資訊發光發熱，這也讓身為助理的你，能透過網路輕鬆做到時尚資料的收集。建議你訂閱 10~15 個國外時尚網站或是時尚部落客的網誌。趁早上通勤或是喝咖啡的時間，每天瀏覽 3~5 個，就能讓你保持與國外潮流同步的敏感度。

UNIT 17 服裝配件的取件與派送安排

Fashion accessories pickup and delivery arrangement

 秘書特助工作內容介紹

　　時尚產業所涵蓋的品項非常廣泛，品牌之間跨界合作的普遍之下，服裝配件或商品之間的往來變成了一種常態。異業合作能讓彼此的目標群眾有交集，產生品牌力互相拉提的作用。特助在協助公司活動的時候，需要負責商借產品，豐富完整活動的主題。時尚業的交流通常是精品的借出與交換，因此相關的配送與商品保管需要由特助來照料。所有精品都需要在活動過程後完整無缺，並安全地運送回異業廠商的手裡，如此相輔相成的合作關係才能穩定發展。

職場上實況對談的一問二答

你有思考過一個品牌形象是背後多少人協力的成果嗎？比方說春夏指甲油的品牌形象呈現，要先找合適的拍攝場地之外，視狀況而定也許需要泳裝、道具、帽子等用品的租借。以下是特助 Amilia 與其他品牌公關 PR 的問答：

Question 1

PR **Hello, Amilia. Thank you for inviting me to this fabulous café to talk over the fashion shoot cooperation. We love your spring-summer nail colors, especially the long-wear edition in ballerina and rouge. And we just have the perfect bikinis to go with them. What style in particular are you looking for?**

你好，愛蜜莉亞，謝謝妳邀請我來這麼棒的咖啡館討論合作案。我們超愛你們這次春夏的指甲的顏色，特別是持久系列的芭蕾舞者和胭脂紅這兩個顏色，跟我們的比基尼會很相稱。請問您想找的泳衣風格是哪一類型呢？

Possible answer 1

A Don't mention it. The pleasure is all mine. I am so glad you have agreed to work with us. We are going for the bohemian beach girl look, so we will love bikini tops and bottoms that we can mix and match. As soon as you are done packing, I will arrange any logistic service that you prefer to pick them up.

別客氣，這是我的榮幸。很高興您同意與我們合作！我們把這季的定位設定在波西米亞海灘女孩，所以我們會需要兩截式的比基尼的上衣和泳褲，讓我們可以混合搭配。等您準備好了，我會安排你指定的物流服務去收件。

Possible answer 2

🅐 You are very welcome. Our new shades of nail color will work best with bold color bikinis. We have also borrowed many giant swimming tubes and pool floats that will make this season's image as colorful and fun as possible. Could you kindly let us know how to handle and care for the swimsuits so that we can keep them in the best condition until we return them to you?

別這麼說，我很樂意。我們新款的指彩色系跟大膽的比基尼色調會最搭。我們還借了許多大型泳圈和充氣船，盡可能讓這一季的形象活潑又鮮艷。您可以指導我們正確的穿用方式嗎？好讓我們把泳裝歸還給你們之前，能讓它們維持最好的狀態。

Question 2

🅟 Hi, Amilia. The logistic service has picked up the swimsuits. You should be getting them soon. As a matter of fact, we will sponsor *SPUR*

magazine's beauty article called "a girl's guide to summer fragrance". We will be sending in vintage swimsuits tomorrow. Would you like to send me a few rosy shades to appear on the article as well?

物流服務已經收件了，你應該很快就會收到包裹了。其實，我們將贊助 SPUR 雜誌的美妝企劃「女孩的夏日香水指南」。明天我會寄送復古風格的泳裝過去給雜誌社，你有興趣送一些薔薇色系的指彩過來，讓產品在雜誌上曝光嗎？

Possible answer 1

Ⓐ Definitely. I will prepare pink nail polish in sweet ballerina, nude pink, and rose quartz for you. I will wrap the packages with bubble wrap so they will be safe during delivery.

當然。我會準備「甜蜜芭蕾舞者」、「透膚粉紅」和「玉石玫瑰」這幾個色系。包裝紙盒外我會再用泡泡紙包裹，確保它們在運送過程中不會受到破壞。

Possible answer 2

Ⓐ Absolutely. I have an ideal product for the fragrance ad. However, it's completely out of stock in the main office. I will arrange a pickup from our dealer near your office and have it delivered to your office today. How does 3 PM sound to you?

當然，我正好有符合這個香水廣告的理想產品。但這商品在總公司是完全缺貨了，我會安排快遞到您附近的經銷商取貨，並在今天把它送到你的辦公室。下午 3 點對您來說方便嗎？

特助補給單字

bohemian *adj.* 波西米亞風格的

logistic *adj.* 物流的

sponsor *v.* 贊助

 秘書特助對答技巧提點

Our new shades of nail color will work best with bold color bikinis.

➲ Work 通常是工作、勞動的意思，但在這裡的意思是合適的涵義。例 1：I don't think this lace top would work with this scarf; besides, we are trying to go for the minimalist look for the season.（我不認為這件蕾絲上衣和這條圍巾可以互搭，除此之外，這季我們想走簡約風。）例 2：The new bag will work with everything; it's the ultimate IT BAG for the year.（這個新款包包是百搭款，堪稱是本年度的經典佳作。）

Could you kindly let us know how to handle and care for the swimsuits so that we can keep them in the best condition until we return them to you?

➲ Could you kindly… 「可以麻煩您……」，這是很禮貌的請求問句。例 1：Could you kindly advise how to dress for a formal occasion?（可以麻煩您建議參加正式場合的時候該如何穿著嗎？）

 秘書特助經驗分享

　　一般包裹的運送，為了爭取時間，通常公司都會有合作的快遞配送公司，以月結的方式，一個月付一次總費用。不過時尚業因為物件的價位都很高，通常會由專人配送，或是自有的物流系統來負責產品的安全。在時尚界異業合作的機會很多，如果不是太忙，建議還是自己將出借的產品送過去，親自與對方見面更能夠延續之後的合作關係喔！

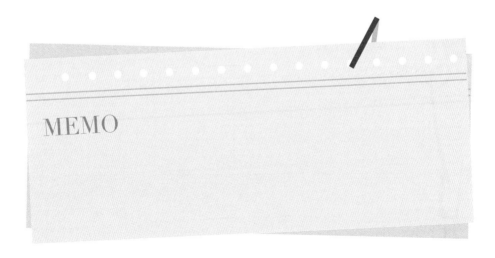

MEMO

時尚攝影工作準備與從旁協助

Fashion shoot setup assistance and preparation

 ## 秘書特助工作內容介紹

　　時尚攝影在時尚界是很重要的環節，因此特助需要有幾個熟識的專業攝影團隊。每個攝影師都有自己擅長的風格與拍攝技巧，你得分辨得出什麼樣的產品該委託哪個攝影團隊。通常攝影師都是獨立工作，隨時都有可能接案子拍攝，因此拍攝的預約也要趁早把握喔！平日多涉獵時尚拍攝的相關作品，若有喜歡的品味與有質感的風格，都可以將攝影師納入自己的合作名單。當然適合拍攝的場地與視覺的掌握，你都要有自己的想法，以便將拍攝的流程與進度確時掌握在你手裡。

職場上實況對談的一問二答 Track 18

負責預約場地、拍攝品項的準備；攝影師、化妝師與模特兒等工作人員的聯絡，以及相關費用的結算都是助理的職責所在。助理不只得扮演著重要的協調者，也得幫忙照料模特兒與導演，因此時尚助理的事前準備與協調能力會左右時尚拍攝順利與否。以下是 Amilia 與攝影團隊 Photo Crew: Marsha 的問答：

Question 1

M Hello, Amilia. This is Marsha from Taiwan Photo Crew. I am calling to confirm your booking on the 23rd, for the fashion party documentation. I would like to discuss the agenda with you. What time are you expecting us on that day?

您好，愛蜜莉亞，我是台灣攝影團隊的瑪莎。我打電話來確認您和我們預約 23 號時尚派對的攝影記錄工作。我想和您討論一下當天的流程。您希望那天我們幾點到呢？

Possible answer 1

A Hello, Marsha. I am so glad that your photo crew has decided to take the job since we adore your work so much. We will invite a lot of our VIPs and popular bloggers to the party, so we would like to give them the red carpet experience. On the day of the party, please be here by 5 PM.

您好，瑪莎，我很高興您的團隊願意接受這份工作，因為我們很喜歡您們作品。我們派對將邀請我們最重要的客戶和很受歡迎的部落客，所以我們想營造走紅星光大道的感覺。那天請在下午 5:00 前到達。

Possible answer 2

Ⓐ Hello, Marsha. Thank you for the confirmation. Let me walk you through the agenda on the day of the party. The party starts at 7pm, so I would like you to be here no later than 6. My boss will give a speech around 7:30. Then there will be art performances and interactions with our guests, so please make sure the party highlights are documented.

瑪莎您好，感謝您的確認。我來講解一下那天的流程。派對是晚上 7 點開始，所以我想您最晚 6 點前要到。我老闆會在 7 點半左右致詞，接下來是文藝表演以及與來賓的互動遊戲，所以請確保這幾個亮點要記錄好。

Question 2

Ⓜ Hi, Amilia. I will need a little more room between the cocktail tables, so I won't be interrupting the guests while I am taking photographs. Also, do you think you can fix the spotlight, so it can focus on the center of the stage?

嗨！愛蜜莉亞，因為我會在這些雞尾酒桌中間走動拍照，所

以我需要多一點空間才不會打擾到客人。另外，你可以調整聚光燈，讓它打在舞台的正中央嗎？

Possible answer 1

🅐 Consider it done. I will have decorators to rearrange the tables and clear out a walkway for you. As for the spotlight, please check if the adjustment is all right.

我會完全照辦。我會請場佈組重新安排桌次，讓你有暢通的走道。聚光燈已經處理了，請現在檢查是否還需要微調。

Possible answer 2

🅐 No problem. I will divide the tables in 2 sections so you will have a walkway in the middle. Can you also go to the second floor to take a panoramic view of the whole party?

沒問題。我會把桌次安排成兩大區，這樣你就可以在中間有一條走道。可以麻煩您上二樓拍派對的全景嗎？

特助補給單字

highlight *n.* 最精彩的部分

spotlight *n.* 聚光燈

秘書特助對答技巧提點

Let me walk you through the agenda on the day of the party.

➲ Walk someone through 這個片語有著很仔細講解，或是從頭到尾指導一遍的意思。例 1：Can you walk me through the return and exchange policy of this brand?（你可以仔細地解說這個品牌的退換貨規則給我聽嗎？）例 2：I will walk you through the procedure of purchasing luxury products on international websites.（我會仔細地教你如何在國際網站上購買奢侈品。）

Then there will be art performances and interactions with our guests, so please make sure the party highlights are documented.

➲ 文中的 highlights 代表著派對中最精彩的部分，也就是藝術表演與互動遊戲的代名詞。例：The highlight of the night will be him proposing to his girlfriend on the center of the stage.（整晚的亮點會是他在舞台上跟他女朋友求婚。）

➲ Be documented 被記錄。例：Her speech on how she turned her blog into her career was documented and was uploaded on YouTube as one of the most popular videos.（她如何把她的部落格轉換成事業的演講被完整地記錄下來，經上傳到 YouTube 後，成為最受歡迎的影片之一。）

秘書特助經驗分享

　　助理在協助產品拍攝的準備過程需要比別人早到，以便先排除場地可能有的問題，拍攝結束還得留下來收尾。但能夠參與精品的拍攝，或是時尚派對的記錄過程，就是你累積實力的機會。過程越是艱辛，狀況越多，你就越快能夠獨當一面。要在時尚業如魚得水，只能透過多年的磨鍊，別無他法。

① 秘書特助篇

② 秘書特助行銷公關篇

MEMO

公司經營問題回報

Operating problems report

 秘書特助工作內容介紹

　　時尚產業必須時刻反映國際潮流的走向，因此新產品的市場接受度、辦公室內部問題回報、競爭對手動態、業績狀況，甚至是員工的心聲等等，特助都需要主動去瞭解情況，並且有能力判斷哪些情報應該及時回報予主管，以免錯過反應的最佳時機。總公司透過各部門主管來確實掌握零售的狀況，然而日理萬機的主管則需要透過特助的協助來獲得許多有利的資訊。一個好的助理，絕不會整日坐辦公室，而是懂得在完成任務之餘，利用時間去作市調與各方情報的搜集。

職場上實況對談的一問二答 Track 19

高階主管經常與基層員工想法大不同，這都是因為中階主管或是特助無法做好溝通或傳達的角色。長期累積下來，可能會造成人才流失或是公司的經營方針無法推動。所以千萬別小看身為特助通報訊息的工作，處理得當是可以促進公司的發展喔！以下是 Ms. Kylie 與特助 Amilia 的問答內容：

Question 1

Ⓚ Hi, Amilia. I notice that you have been going to our branch stores from time to time. Do you have any feedback for me?

嗨！愛蜜莉亞，我有注意到你常會去分店看看，你有什麼意見可以提供給我嗎？

Possible answer 1

Ⓐ I was just about to report to you. I found that each store has its own style of product arrangements and window displays. Although localization is very important, I still think a unified brand image is the key.

我正要向您匯報呢。我發現每家店都有自己的產品陳列方式和不同風格的窗口佈置。雖然在地化很重要，但我仍然認為不能捨棄一致的品牌形象。

Possible answer 2

🅐 Yes, Ms. Kylie. When I was in some of our retail stores, I felt like they didn't take advantage of making a connection to our customers. If visiting the store is down to transaction only, our stores don't offer much advantage over online stores.

是的，凱莉小姐，當我在逛我們的零售據點時，我覺得店員沒有利用機會與客戶接觸。如果逛商店只剩買賣，我們的分店比起網路商店並沒有更大的優勢。

Question 2

🅚 **Amilia, apparel inventory management has been the worsening problem of the fashion industry. We need to deal with the issue before it becomes a problem for us. Speaking of which, have you heard anything from Marketing and Sales?**

愛蜜莉亞，服裝的庫存管理一直是時尚界顯現的問題，我們需要預先處理，以預防這個問題的出現。說到這個，妳最近有從行銷部和業務部聽到什麼消息嗎？

Possible answer 1

🅐 Due to the economic constrain, consumers are more sensitive to price setting. Marketing has been striving to promote multiple channels, such as social media, online stores and forum discussions. Our fashion products tend to be seasonal and have a short lifespan. We will need more precise sales data to monitor our consumer habits so that we can make better purchase decisions.

由於經濟的限制，消費者對價格變得更敏感。行銷部一直在努力推動多重通路的行銷，例如社交媒體、網路商店和論壇等。我們的時尚品項往往有季節性，產品壽命很短，我們需要更精準的銷售數據來監測消費者習慣，讓我們可以做出更好的產品購買決策。

Possible answer 2

A Yes. In order to reduce inventory, Marketing has suggested broadening our customer reach by collaborating with other brands or artists, so that we can have bigger share of the market. The Sales Department has put their sales representatives in new training seminars to advance their ability to connect with consumers and provide better customer services.

是的，為了減少庫存，行銷部已經建議要和其他品牌或藝術家合作，以擴大我們的客戶範圍。這樣我們可以擁有更大的市佔率。業務部門已經安排銷售代表參加全新的培訓研討會，加強他們與消費者建立關係的能力，並提供更好的客戶服務。

特助補給單字

localization *n.* 在地化

unify *v.* 使相同

transaction *n.* 買賣

precise *adj.* 精準的

 秘書特助對答技巧提點

I notice that you have been going to our branch stores from time to time. Do you have any feedback for me?

➔ from time to time 是很常見的片語用法，這個時間代名詞有著「偶爾」或是「每過一段時間」的意思。例：I go to New York from time to time for old time's sake.（我每過一段時間就會回去紐約，重溫以前的好時光。）

Due to the economic constrain, consumers are more sensitive to price setting.

➔ Due to... 是因為……的意思，可以放句首或句中來使用。例：Due to the earthquake, our trip to the factory is postponed.（因為地震的關係，我們去工廠出差的行程暫緩。）；Be sensitive to... 受某事物影響或對某事物感到警覺。例：My boss is very sensitive to political issues; it's best if we stay away from the topic to avoid any confrontation.（我老闆對於政治話題很敏感,我們最好別討論這類的話題以免引起紛爭。）

秘書特助經驗分享

　　提醒主管公司內部出了問題會需要點勇氣,因為公司高層對於經營管理的看法,與基層員工的考量點的確很難一致。以女主管來說,不建議在會議上提出看法,而是在私底下兩人討論的時候,以求助的角度來徵詢對方的意見。男性主管較為果斷,提出問題的時候,你最好已經想好幾個解決方法來請對方裁示,而不是單純的請求協助。

MEMO

營運費用報告製作與預算審核
Production of office expense report and review

 秘書特助工作內容介紹

　　上一個章節提到三大文書處理軟體的 Word 與 Excel。Excel 是做預算報表的好幫手，能夠幫助你快速將數據表格化，還可以加總、分析，並且圖像化等功能。時尚產業的營運費相當多元化，例如出差國外採購一趟下來，會有食宿、交通、展覽門票或交際應酬等費用。辦公室的營運費用除了文具之外，會有快遞費、樣品打樣、咖啡茶點，甚至是美化辦公室的植栽等等。將營運費用清楚地表現在報表上，方便主管作出正確的判斷，是身為特助很重要的職責之一喔！

職場上實況對談的一問二答　 Track 20

通常營運預算做出來會先由財務部作審核，財務長同意之後，視公司狀況而定，有時候是以部門先代墊，之後再按照預算報表跟公司請款。你也可以跟公司先預支費用，之後再按照收據與實際費用，多退少補。以下是特助 Amilia 與財務部 Paul 之間的問答：

Question 1

P Hi, Amilia. I got your message about the expense report on your trip to Milan. I understand that you have some questions to ask before you compose it?

嗨，愛蜜莉亞，我有收到妳的訊息。據我所知，妳想在製作米蘭出差開支報告之前，先問我一些問題是嗎？

Possible answer 1

A Hi, Paul. Thanks for calling. Yes, I am a little bit confused about the expense report format since all the calculations will be done in US dollars, but I will actually be using Euros on the trip. Could you kindly let me know my spending limit as an assistant, as well as the approval cycle?

您好，保羅，謝謝您主動撥電話過來。我的確對費用報告的格式感到有一點點困惑，因為所有的計算會以美元為基準，但我出差的時候，事實上會使用歐元。你可以讓我知道，以

助理的權限，出差的消費額度是多少呢？還有費用審核的流程，需要經過哪些人？

Possible answer 2

🅐 Yes. However, I just realized the web-based expense report program has rate conversion support, which would be easy for me to switch from Euros to US dollars. I can just input all the Euro expenses in one column, and the total amount will be added and converted into US dollars. I will be able to update the expense report while I travel, and approvers can track my expenses whenever they want. How convenient!

是的，不過我後來發現網路版的開支報告有匯率轉換的功能，這樣我可以很方便地將歐元轉成美元。我可以只輸入所有的歐元開支在欄位裡，總金額就會自動加總，並兌換成美元。我也可以在旅行的時候隨時更新費用報告，費用審核者也可以馬上追蹤我的費用。真是方便呢！

Question 2

🅿 Amilia, the expense report of the pop-up shop in the weekend market looks pretty good to me. Here you include all the vendors, expense categories, the amount and receipts in chronological order. May I ask if this is for the

evaluation of the activity or just for reimbursement?

嗨！愛蜜莉亞，週末市場短期店鋪的費用報告看起來很不錯。你已經按時間順序列出所有的供應商、支出類別、金額和收據。請問這個營運費用報表只是要評價活動的效益，還是用來核銷使用呢？

Possible answer 1

🄰 You read my mind, Paul. I am preparing the expense report to compare the amount of investment we put in and see if it is reflected on the profit of the event or not.

保羅你簡直太瞭解我了。我準備這個營運費用報告是要用來比較我們的投資額，並看看這些投資是否反映在營業額上。

Possible answer 2

🄰 Actually, it is just for accounting purposes. This is also a complete record in the pricing of all the hardware and woodwork, as well as installing and display service charges throughout the event in case we need it for future references and other expense analysis.

其實這只是要交給會計作帳使用。這也是活動中所有硬體和木製品訂價、安裝費用和陳列佈置等服務費的完整記錄。如果未來有需要，可以用來參考使用或是製作費用分析。

特助補給單字

compose *v.* 組成、構圖

chronological *adj.* 按照時間順序的

 秘書特助對答技巧提點

Could you kindly let me know my spending limit as an assistant?

○ as an assistant 以助理角色／身為一個助理。As... 指身為……／作為某種身份的代表。例 1：As a manager, I have responsibility to train my team members and motivate them to achieve higher sales record. （身為一名經理，我有責任訓練我的團隊，鼓勵他們實現更高的銷售記錄。）

I will be able to update the expense report while I travel, and approvers can track my expenses whenever they want.

○ Update 更新，也能用於表達「定期報告」的概念。例 1：Please update our customers' data at least once a day; each customer who comes in our shop is a valuable asset to our company. （請至少每天更新一次我們的客戶資料，每一位來店的客戶都是我們公司非常重視的資

產。）例 2：You need to <u>update</u> the sales data and report to Accounting everyday because we generate a sales report every Monday before each sales meeting. （你需要每天報告銷售數字給會計部，為了因應業務會議，每週一都會出一次銷售報表。）

 秘書特助經驗分享

　　辦公室的營運費用報告，通常是由特助或秘書來完成。該報告記錄著一個月營運所需要的雜項支出，而部門主管則可視費用的增減，來調整營運模式。營運費用報告一定不能有錯誤，所以發票與收據的保管也要很仔細。盡量養成隨時作記錄的好習慣，累積一整個月的費用記錄後再對帳容易發生錯誤，也必定會浪費時間回想費用產生的日期。

MEMO

UNIT 21 人員應徵協助
Recruiting assistance

 秘書特助工作內容介紹

　　員工的應徵是透過人力資源部，但助理必須列出求職者的職能需求給 Human Resources (HR)，才能精確選到合適的人選。助理最瞭解辦公室的狀況，對於應徵新人的協助也是責無旁貸。面試約談間的聯繫、給予部分的員工訓練、同事與環境介紹與等職責，都會交由助理來完成。這過程當中的聯絡與接待，會左右新進人員的感受與對公司的印象，進而影響新進人員留在公司的意願。耗費太多資源在應徵人員或是員工訓練的循環當中，是很多時尚產業面臨到的問題之一。

職場上實況對談的一問二答 Track 21

職員汰換率（Employment turnover）很高的公司，不但人力成本增加，也會影響在職員工的心情，減弱員工對公司的向心力。身為特助，你可以幫助人資，有效率地刻劃出部門所需人選的人格特質與工作能力，有效降低新進員工對部門可能會有的不適應。以下是特助 Amilia 與人力資源部 Leah 的問答：

Question 1

🄛 Hello, Amilia. I have got the request form for merchandiser recruitment that you have submitted. Do you mind giving me more information about the job position that you are trying to fill?

妳好，愛蜜莉亞，我收到了妳提交的採購人員招聘申請表。妳可以幫我多瞭解這個需要人遞補的職位嗎？

Possible answer 1

🄐 Hey, Leah. Of course, I would love to talk to you about it. Well, since one of our merchandisers is leaving in a month, we need someone who is experienced in working with suppliers and capable of choosing the potential fashion couture in the right quantities at the right price.

妳好，利亞，當然沒問題。我很樂意和妳談談這件事喔！我們其中一個採購再一個月就要離開了，所以我們需要一位與

131

供應商交涉多年的人才，並能以合適的價格與數量採購具有
潛力的時尚服飾。

Possible answer 2

🅐 Hello, Leah. Thank you for meeting me. I would be happy to talk to you about it. We need a merchandiser who will be eager to analyze the past sales figures, anticipating future fashion trends and consumer needs. He or she also needs to advise a contract with the vendors and ensure the quality control and product accuracy in order to minimize inventory stocks.

妳好，利亞，謝謝妳特地跑一趟，我很開心可以跟妳討論這
件事。我們需要的採購必須樂於分析過去的銷售數據、並對
預測未來流行趨勢和消費者的需求充滿熱誠。還需要建立與
供應商的合約，以控制產品的質感與運送商品的準確度，以
盡量減少庫存為目標。

Question 2

🅛 Hi, Amilia. I understand that your department wants to hire a new merchandiser. I've got quite a few resumes coming in this week. I am going to need you to help me narrow down the candidates; do you have a minute now?

嗨，愛蜜莉亞，我知道妳們部門要聘請新的採購，這週我收

到了不少的履歷。我需要妳幫我挑選出最適合的人選，妳現在有空嗎？

Possible answer 1

🅐 Yes, I do. Okay, the merchandiser we are looking for will need to be involved in setting the price and work under pressure since he or she is dealing with turnover in many stores.

我現在正好有空。好，我們正在尋找的採購必須要參與定價，抗壓力要好，因為他需要負責許多商店的營業額。

Possible answer 2

🅐 Certainly. The merchandiser we are hiring will need at least 5 years in the field. Additionally, he or she needs profound statistics skills to determine trends and potential risks and opportunities. He or she will need to be confident when it comes to communication and negotiation.

當然沒問題，我們正在招聘的人才將需要在時尚領域擁有最少五年的採購經驗，另外，他得具備優秀的統計能力以預測未來趨勢，以及潛在的風險和機會。他或她要對溝通和談判充滿自信。

特助補給單字

recruitment *n.* 徵才

potential *adj.* 有潛力的

candidate *n.* 人選

merchandiser *n.* 採購

 秘書特助對答技巧提點

We need a merchandiser who will be eager to analyze the past sales figures, anticipating future fashion trends and consumer needs.

➲ Eager 熱切的。此字有兩個比較常見的用法：eager to V 或 eager for N。文章內所提到的用法，就是屬於第一種。例 1：She is eager to apply for a design school and start her own brand.（她很渴望申請設計學院，並邁向她的自創品牌之路。）例 2：After 10 years in this law firm without a promotion, she is eager for a change.（在這個律師事務所待了 10 年還沒有升職，她很渴望生活能有點改變。）

We need someone who is experienced in working with suppliers and capable of choosing the potential fashion couture in the right quantities at the right price.

➲ Be capable of 有能力處理，或具有某種能力。使用公式為 「of＋Ving」。任何介系詞後面加上動詞都要改成原形動詞 ＋ing，把動詞轉化成名詞，文法才是正確的喔！例 1：I am capable of setting up a 200 people wedding in a month.（我可以在一個月內籌備好可以容納 200 人的婚禮。）例 2：When she is in a good mood, she is capable of anything.（她心情好的時候，可以勝任任何困難的狀況。）

 ## 秘書特助經驗分享

　　與時尚界相關的工作項目除了採購之外，還有品牌行銷、品牌業務、廣告設計、時尚編輯、媒體、設計師與服裝師等琳琅滿目的工作內容。如果你對某個領域感到興趣，你應該先進到時尚產業實習開始。就算不是本科系出身也無妨，只要紮實地累積專業，還是很有機會可以轉職成功的！

秘書特助篇 ❶

秘書特助行銷公關篇 ❷

UNIT 22 督導新進員工

Training and supervising junior staff

 秘書特助工作內容介紹

　　上一個章節提到助理需要在人員招募的時候提供協助，待新人進公司後，助理依然要負起指導的工作責任喔！人力資源部所提供的員工訓練，只限於公司規章與員工基本的權利與義務。新人被分配到新的工作崗位時，每個辦公室都會有潛規則，因此助理必須要充當前輩，給予新進人員指導與鼓勵。新人越快適應公司，也就能越快把分內的工作做好。時尚產業的步調快，競爭又激烈，如果缺乏人帶領訣竅，問題時常無法獲得解決的話，很容易造成新人快速退場。

職場上實況對談的一問二答   Track 22

新進員工訓練（Employee orientation）能讓新進員工理解公司期待的工作態度與價值觀。而時尚產業因為步調快，辦公室環境容易產生壓力與衝突，而適當的員工訓練能幫助員工排解工作上的問題並有助於人際關係。以下是 Amilia 與新進員工 Noah 的問答：

Question 1

Ⓝ **Hello, Amilia. Thank you for introducing me to everyone in the office and the orientation tour of the office facilities. I was wondering if there are social activities or sports clubs that you would suggest if I want to meet more people within the company?**

您好，愛蜜莉亞，謝謝您講解辦公室設施，還有介紹大家給我認識。您可以告訴我，公司是否有社交活動或體育社團，好讓我在公司可以盡快認識更多的人呢？

Possible answer 1

Ⓐ Noah. That's a great question! We have a very popular badminton club and it has practice every Wednesday if you are interested. Human Resources also updates club information once a month.

諾亞，這是個好問題！我們有非常受歡迎的羽毛球社。如果你有興趣的話，他們固定每星期三練習。人力資源每個月更

新社團訊息。

Possible answer 2

🅐 That's a great idea. In fact, we have a group outing once a month and we are going salsa dancing next week! The funding comes from 1% of our paycheck and the rest comes from the company's welfare foundation.

這是一個好主意。事實上，我們每個月都會出遊，下週我們要去學薩爾薩舞！這些費用來自於我們每個月薪資扣除的百分之一，其餘的補助來自於公司的福利基金會。

Question 2

🅝 **Hey, Amilia. Thank you for being so helpful in my first week here. I would like to know the guidelines in the office, so I can get along with everyone here.**

嗨！愛蜜莉亞，謝謝您在我來的第一個禮拜這麼照顧我。我想問您這個辦公室的規矩，我希望可以和大家和平相處。

Possible answer 1

🅐 That's very considerate of you, Noah. I just want you to know that we are all very happy to have you here. Our offices get really busy at the end of each month, so if you are done with your work early, you can ask around if anyone needs assistance. We are a small office, so lending a hand when it's needed would be a great relief.

諾亞，你真的很貼心。我只是想讓你知道，我們都非常高興你來這裡上班。我們辦公室每個月底都很忙，所以如果你手上的工作已經做完了，你可以打聽一下，是否有人需要幫助。我們辦公室規模不大，所以任何幫助都會讓我們覺得輕鬆很多。

Possible answer 2

Ⓐ Thank you for asking. We all want you to fit in here, so don't be afraid to ask questions. You are allowed to make mistakes in the first month. The fashion industry can be stressful sometimes, so we appreciate a positive attitude, it really lightens the mood in the office.

謝謝你的關心。我們都希望你能適應這裡，所以不要害怕問問題。你來的第一個月錯誤是可以被接受的。時尚界有時候很緊繃，所以我們讚賞積極正面的態度，能讓大家在辦公室的心情保持良好。

▌特助補給單字

facility *n.* 設備

paycheck *n.* 薪資

relief *n.* 解圍

秘書特助對答技巧提點

We are a small office, so lending a hand when it's needed would be a great relief.

➲ Lend a hand or lend someone a hand 是伸出援手或是幫忙的意思。例 1：Could you lend me a hand with this marketing research?（你可以協助我蒐集市場調查的資料嗎？）例 2：In our house, children are expected to lend a hand when it's needed.（在我們家小孩一定要幫忙做家事。）

That's very considerate of you, Noah.

➲ Be considerate of someone 對某人體貼，或對某人周到。另外也有「considerate to V」這個用法。例 1：It's very considerate of you as a kindergarten teacher to give the children and parents who have separation anxiety some time to adjust.（你這位幼稚園老師真的很體貼，給了孩子和有分離恐懼症的家長們一些時間調適。）例 2：He was considerate enough to inform me that he will be leaving the company in 3 months.（他很體貼地提前通知我，再三個月他就要離職了。）

秘書特助經驗分享

　　一個時尚助理的雜事很多，所以你很有可能有機會碰到新進人員來分擔你的工作。建議一開始先不要把對外聯絡的工作交給他，可以先交接文書處理、跑腿、跑公司流程的工作。這些工作就算出錯，也能夠馬上改正過來。你可以觀察他是否細心、是否擅長與人相處，到時候再把大一點的專案交給他處理也不遲。

❶ 秘書特助篇

❷ 秘書特助行銷公關篇

MEMO

參與公司福利委員會

Participating in the welfare committee

 秘書特助工作內容介紹

　　福利委員會每年都會改選會員，目的就是希望讓員工輪流爭取自己喜歡的回饋活動。每年一到台灣習俗的三節：農曆年、端午與中秋節，福委會都會開會表決每個節日的禮品選項。台灣企業重視的尾牙，其中的表演節目與獎項準備，也都是由福利委員會（Welfare Committee）來籌備的喔！沒錯，助理一定得列席參加，除了需要回報主管之外，也得幫忙處理經費統計與記帳、採購，以及廠商之間的溝通協調。社團與員工旅遊也屬福委會的範疇，把這些活動辦好，是你練習規劃與發揮能力的好機會！

職場上實況對談的一問二答　Track 23

參加福委會的活動是義務為大家服務，在老闆的眼裡是充滿熱誠的好員工，在同事間是熱心公益。大家為了自己的權益會主動向你問問題，助理也就能在這時候，當大家的好幫手，與大家之間的距離也會拉近。以下是時尚業特助 Amilia 與同事 Camilla 的問答：

Question 1

ⓒ Thank you for holding the welfare committee meeting today, so we are going to discuss the company trip in winter, right?

謝謝妳召開福委會議，所以我們今天要討論冬季的員工旅遊對吧？

Possible answer 1

Ⓐ Yes, we are. I have talked to the travel agency yesterday and discussed a few options about the travel agenda. We will hire a French Fashion consultant who's based in Tokyo; she will introduce the fashion industry in Tokyo, so we can observe the overseas market trend. Now we just have to narrow things down, so we don't go over our budget.

沒錯，我昨天已經跟旅行社討論出幾個旅遊選項。我們會聘請駐點東京的法國時尚顧問。她會為我們介紹東京的時尚

界，我們可以觀摩海外市場的走向。現在我們只需要縮小參觀的範圍，讓我們不至於超出預算。

Possible answer 2

A Indeed, we are planning to hire a fashion insider from Tokyo; we will be browsing through stylish boutiques and districts in Harajuku, Aoyama, and Shibuya and so on. The trip will be exciting, out of ordinary, and it will also help us improve our visual merchandising and display.

我們計劃要聘請一位東京的時尚顧問，他會帶領我們參訪原宿、青山和澀谷等地區的精品店，一探東京的時尚內幕。這次的旅程出奇制勝，很令人期待，它也將幫助我們在視覺行銷和陳列方面的技能。

Question 2

C **Our corporate message this year is "family," so perhaps we can plan a year-end party that can include our whole family. Do you have a party theme in mind?**

我們公司今年的企業訊息是以「家庭」為核心，所以也許我們可以舉辦一個全家都能參與的尾牙活動。妳現在心裡有理想的尾牙主題嗎？

Possible answer 1

A Yes, I do, actually. Outdoor activities such as

picnics are very popular right now. I was thinking an English royal tea party that includes a horse carriage. It could be fun for both our employees and family members.

我其實有個想法。最近戶外野餐的活動很盛行。我想幫我們的員工和家屬舉辦一個有馬車的英國皇室下午茶。

Possible answer 2

Ⓐ I have absolutely no clue; I was hoping we could all pitch in with some ideas together. If we want to invite the family members of our employees to join our year-end party, we need to consider locations that are suitable for children and the elderly.

我完全沒有頭緒。所以我希望大家能一起發想。如果我們想邀請員工家屬參加我們的年終晚會,我們需要考慮適合兒童和長者的場所。

▌特助補給單字

consultant *n.* 顧問

narrow *v.* 縮小範圍

insider *n.* 消息靈通的人

royal *adj.* 皇家的

秘書特助對答技巧提點

We will hire a French Fashion consultant who's based in Tokyo; she will introduce the fashion industry in Tokyo, so we can observe the overseas market trend.

➲ Be based in… 某人／公司駐點在某地……。例 1：Our main company is based in Germany; however, our factory is in France, and we have branch offices all over the world. （我們總公司駐點在德國，但工廠在法國，而我們在世界各地都設有分公司。）例 2：She was working in Taiwan, but after the promotion, she is now based in Hong Kong, supervising the branch office and travels once a month for corporate meetings. （她本來在台灣工作，但升職後她被派駐在香港管理分公司，每個月回總公司開一次會。）

Now we just have to narrow things down, so we don't go over our budget.

➲ Narrow down 片語：縮小範圍。例：We are willing to burn the midnight oil as long as we can narrow down the list of the items we are purchasing for the new season. （我們寧願挑燈夜戰，只要可以順利縮減我們下一季訂單的採購項目。）

秘書特助經驗分享

　　福利金的來源除了企業按照政府機關規定的提撥金額外，還有每個月從員工薪水中提撥的 **0.5%**。這是身為勞工的權益，不要白白地讓它流失囉！最好的監督方式，就是參加福委會了，你可以實際參與福利事項的選擇，對福利金的帳目清楚，你才能知道公司是否有確實執行義務。

MEMO

組織團隊向心力活動

Organizing team building activities

秘書特助工作內容介紹

　　許多企業會利用週末在度假村舉行兩天一夜的會議，第一天開完會後大家就可以放鬆休閒，目的就是要讓員工之間的人際關係更緊密。有時候透過運動會或是義工活動，是一種促進團體榮譽感與信任感的方式，既健康也正面。時尚界當然也不例外，只是活動內容會多加入美感培養的元素，例如參觀畫展或是接觸大自然的洗禮。時尚界的助理經常得協辦 corporate team building，重點在於要寓教於樂，讓員工願意自動自發地參與，公司也能順帶做教育訓練，雙方都能皆大歡喜。

職場上實況對談的一問二答　

如果藉由公司舉辦的團體活動，可以增加專業知識、拓展眼界，同時又能旅遊，這樣正面的活動最能有效凝聚員工對公司的向心力。時尚界很多精品都是手工製造的品項，參觀工廠的製造流程，不但能加強員工介對產品的了解，也能激發創造力。以下是員工 Milo 與特助 Amilia 之間的問答：

Question 1

Ⓜ **Hey, Amilia. I would like to inform my team to keep their agendas open for the team building activity. Therefore, could you give me more details about the trip?**

愛蜜莉亞妳好，我想先通知我的組員，讓他們把時間空下來參加公司團隊建設的活動。所以妳可以給我比較詳細的行程嗎？

Possible answer 1

Ⓐ Hey, Milo. How are you? Team building will be a 2-day trip. On the first day, we will visit the bamboo-weaving factory to learn about the Taiwanese traditional weaving techniques. We will also participate in weaving a basket, so all of us will get a souvenir to take home. Then we are staying one night at the bamboo sanctuary where the serene and fresh air will help us unwind after the entire season of hard work.

嗨，米洛，你好嗎？團隊建立會是兩天一夜的行程。第一天會參觀竹子編織工廠，了解台灣傳統編織技術。我們也會參加編織竹籃的活動，這樣我們都會有紀念品可以帶回家。當天晚上會在竹林保護區過夜，那裡的寧靜和清新的空氣可以幫助我們放鬆打拼一整季的疲憊。

Possible answer 2

Ⓐ Not a problem, Milo. I was just about to send out an e-mail about team building. Anyhow, on November 24ᵗʰ, the whole company will join an ice sculpting class. We will all split into several groups; each group will have 4 or 5 people and watch a demonstration by a professional ice sculptor. Each group will take charge of planning, designing, and building the ice sculpture of their own.

沒問題，米洛。我正準備要發送一封關於團隊建設的電子郵件。總之，11 月 24 日全公司會參加冰塊雕刻的課程。我們會把大家分成 4 或 5 人小組，先觀賞專業冰雕老師的示範。每個小組會負責規劃、設計和創作自己的冰雕。

Question 2

Ⓜ **Hey, Amilia. I heard we might be having another team building activity next month. We are very excited since the last ice sculpting team**

bonding activity was such a success. Can we try an outdoor activity this time?

嗨！愛蜜莉亞，聽說我們下個月可能會有團隊建立的活動。我們都很期待，因為上一次的冰雕活動很成功，這次我們是不是可以嘗試戶外活動呢？

Possible answer 1

Ⓐ Hello, Milo. Thanks for your suggestion. I was thinking the same thing! I've been talking to a women's community in the East of Taiwan. They are in need of bee hive frames as a second source of family income. We can volunteer to build beehives and donate those to the community, so they can produce honey, beeswax, and turn them into other products.

您好，米洛，感謝您的建議。我也正有此意呢！我最近跟台東的婦女團體常有聯絡，她們需要製作蜂箱為家庭增加第二個收入來源。我們可以義務性建造蜂箱並捐贈給社區，讓他們能夠生產蜂蜜和蜂蠟，並製作其他副產品。

Possible answer 2

Ⓐ Hi, Milo. Thank you for putting so much thought into the subject. I was actually considering an outdoor treasure hunt adventure.

你好，米洛，謝謝你花這麼多心思在這主題上。我其實有考慮要舉辦戶外探險尋寶的活動。

特助補給單字

weaving *n.* 編織

sanctuary *n.* 保護區

unwind *v.* 放鬆

beeswax *n.* 蜂蠟

 秘書特助對答技巧提點

Then we are staying one night at the bamboo sanctuary where the serene and fresh air will help us unwind after the entire season of hard work.

➲ Where 在這裡是關係代名詞的用法，用以代替 the bamboo sanctuary 這個地點。Where 只能代替地方名詞，或是不同大小的區域都可以，不能代替人或事。例：Taiwan is a beautiful country where you can appreciate distinct sceneries in all four seasons. （台灣是一個美麗的國家，在那裡你可以欣賞四季不同的風景。）

We will all split into several groups; each group will have 4 or 5 people and watch a demonstration by a professional ice sculptor.

➲ Split into 這個片語的意思是：……把……分成幾人／份／隊。例 1：Please split this bucket of flowers into 6 bouquets and send them to each one of our dealers. （請把這款桶鮮花分成 6 把花束，再一一送給我們的經銷商。）例 2：This project <u>can be split into</u> 5 categories, so all our team members can help out.（這個專案可以被分成 5 大項目，這樣一來我們所有的團隊成員都可以出一份力。）

秘書特助經驗分享

公司內的競賽也可以被當成 team building 的活動之一喔！比賽不但能夠激起員工的鬥志，也可以促進組員間的合作。畢竟 team building 的意義在於團隊的組織，只要能凝結團隊的向心力，又是對公司有益的活動，無論是比賽業績、唱歌或是拉拉隊舞蹈都是可以被接受的。如果今天你是負責舉辦 team building 的總召，你會想出怎樣的活動呢？

MEMO

PART 2
秘書特助行銷公關篇

Marketing/ public relations job profiles
in the fashion industry

行銷策略

Marketing strategies

 ## 秘書特助工作內容介紹

　　只要行銷手法能啟動消費者對產品的渴望，時尚產業的行銷策略沒有限制，這也是為什麼很多廣告界的經典之作都來自於時尚界。設計師將華麗的思想成就為一項商品，賣的也許遠超過這個商品的工藝或質料；賣的可能是設計師的名氣、品牌的價值與廣告創造的美好憧憬等附加價值。如果你有幸加入一個很棒的團隊，也就是擁有能夠互相鼓舞、啟發靈感的同事，他們必須能夠坦誠地提出意見與批評，這樣的團隊所激盪出來的行銷策略才有可能感動人心。

職場上實況對談的一問二答　 Track 25

時尚產業與藝術有著密不可分的關係，但身為行銷你必須要非常清楚你要推廣的是時尚事業還是藝術美學，因為這將會強烈影響到銷售的形象與方式。你必須要瞭解你的群眾，甚至是創造你的群眾，你的行銷策略才可能奏效。以下是 Amilia 與時尚設計師 Tom 之間的問答：

Question 1

T After adjusting our pricing policy, our sales have gone up 10 percent. I think it is time to focus on our long-term strategies to direct our brand in a better direction. How about we start with the advertising campaign?

在調整我們的訂價策略之後，銷售數字已經上升了百分之十。我覺得現在是時候調整我們的長期行銷戰略，讓品牌可以往更好的方向發展。不如我們先從廣告活動開始吧？

Possible answer 1

A Great idea! As we are trying to attract the younger generation, perhaps we could move away from a product-oriented advertisement to a brand associated advertisement. We want to present a vision of fashion and creativity that our customers want to be part of.

好主意！我們現在要盡全力吸引年輕的消費族群，以往的廣告模式都是以產品為主，也許我們能改以品牌導向。我們想展示時尚和創意的理念，讓我們的客戶希望成為其中的一份子。

Possible answer 2

🅐 Absolutely. After a careful marketing survey, we have gotten a lot of positive feedback about you. Instead of hiring a celebrity for our brand image, why not promote our own designer?

當然，經過仔細的市場調查後，我們發現你的形象得到了很多正面的回饋。與其僱用一個名人作為我們的品牌形象，何不宣傳我們自家的設計師？

Question 2

🅣 The world of fashion is my passion. If your marketing team thinks I am the best person for the brand image, I am more than happy to help. However, that's only a fraction of the entire marketing strategy. What's next?

時尚世界是我的熱情所在，如果行銷團隊認為我是為品牌形象的最佳人選，我樂意之至。然而，這只是行銷策略的一部分，下一步呢？

Possible answer 1

Ⓐ Aside from the designer promotion, I would also like to emphasize our fine craftsmanship and our relationship with independent factories in Italy. We want to remind our target audience that our brand represents sophisticated styles and top quality.

除了設計師的推廣行銷，我也想強調我們精湛的工藝，以及我們與義大利小型獨立工廠的良好關係。我們想要提醒我們的目標群眾，我們的品牌代表了精緻的風格和品質保證。

Possible answer 2

Ⓐ A part of reinventing the brand image and corporate message to the market includes managing our product distribution. The younger generation needs shopping experiences that are interactive and edgy. Visiting our distribution channels should be exciting and rewarding. We want to control how the market perceives the brand by effective advertising and channel marketing.

部分的品牌形象和企業訊息的重整包括管理產品的通路行銷。年輕一代所需要的購物體驗是前衛並具有互動性的，到我們分店的經驗應該是令人期待並有所收獲的。我們要透過有效的廣告視覺和通路行銷來控制這個品牌給市場的形象。

特助補給單字

vision *n.* 願景

fraction *n.* 片段

strategy *n.* 策略

audience *n.* 聽眾

 秘書特助對答技巧提點

Perhaps we could move away from a product-oriented advertisement to a brand associated advertisement.

➲ N＋oriented 指某種定位，或朝某個目標發展。例：He is a very goal-oriented person. I don't think anyone could take his mind away from work.（他是非常目標導向的人，我覺得沒有人有辦法讓他從工作分心。）

I would also like to emphasize our fine craftsmanship and our relationship with independent factories in Italy.

➲ Emphasize 強調是及物動詞，後面可以直接加受詞，如果後面要加上一段句子，也可以先加上「that」來引導。例 1：Our company emphasizes social responsibilities and animal welfare.（我們公司很重視社會責任與動物福利。）例 2：In our culture, we emphasize that elderly relatives shall not to be left alone at home and have to be well taken care of.（在我們的文化裡，我們強調年老的親屬，不能被單獨留在家中，並且要得到妥善的照顧。）

秘書特助經驗分享

就像人生規劃一樣，品牌的行銷策略也有短期和長期目標。最重要的是先掌握品牌的願景，思考你對品牌有怎樣的發展與期許？你希望品牌發展到多大的經濟規模？是否推廣產品到全球？在長期的計畫中，你甚至得準備退場或轉型的機制。先擬出計劃書後，以品牌的願景為中心，隨著品牌的發展，你可以隨著新目標或市場的變動來修正行銷策略。

MEMO

市場分析

Marketing analysis

 秘書特助工作內容介紹

　　優秀的市場分析報告，來自於精準的目標族群與縝密的市場調查，這兩個要點缺一不可。通常在推出新品之前，應該要先進行市場分析，找出市場的需求，給予研發或是產品經理新品成立的方向。市場分析也可以利用在採購上，分析的結果可以幫助預測市場的購買意願。在創造需求與發展新客群的時候，市場分析也總是能幫助行銷團隊去勾勒出具有戰力的行銷策略。時尚業的市場分析（Market Analysis）也包括國外市調與流行訊息分析，對於行銷和業務都能是十分有利的消息。

職場上實況對談的一問二答

市場調查的手法有很多種，包含市場觀察（observation）、問卷調查（survey）和焦點團體和產品試用調查（focus group and product testing）等。你可以依據產品與品牌的特性去選擇適用的市場調查方式。以下是行銷專員 Amilia 與參與市場調查者 participant 之間的問答：

Question 1

🅟 **This is my first time participating in a focus group. Could you kindly explain the difference between a focus group and a regular meeting?**

這是我第一次參加一個焦點小組，可以請您解釋一下「焦點小組」和其它的小組有什麼不一樣嗎？

Possible answer 1

🅐 First of all, thank you all for being here. The difference between a focus group and a regular meeting is that we have a specific discussion topic, which is our new advertising campaign. A focus group is highly structured, so I will be your facilitator today, and I am here to actively encourage you to express your opinions.

首先感謝大家來到這裡。焦點小組和一般會議之間最大的區別是我們有一個特定的討論話題，也就是我們最新的廣告企劃。焦點團體很重視組織與程序，所以我會擔任主持人，在

163

這裡積極鼓勵各位表達意見。

Possible answer 2

A That is a great question! You have been carefully selected to join our focus group because your profile fits what we want for our target audience. Therefore, anything you say in this group meeting is greatly appreciated. We have conducted a written survey prior to the focus group, and now we are looking forward to your verbal statement, so we can also get your thoughts and feelings towards our topic.

這是一個很好的問題！各位是我們精心挑選出的小組成員，因為您們的背景資料符合我們的目標群眾。因此各位在這個焦點會議上所說的一切，對我們來說都是很寶貴的意見。我們之前已經進行過問卷調查，現在我們期待的是各位的發言，這樣我們才能更瞭解您的想法和感受。

Question 2

P Hi, I am here for the focus group for product testing. I am not sure if I am in the right building, could you kindly tell me which way to go?

您好，我是來參加產品測試的焦點小組，我不確定我是不是走對大樓了，您能告訴我該往哪邊走嗎？

Possible answer 1

Ⓐ Welcome, and right this way. Here is a questionnaire with a few questions about the new product. You can also use it to write down your notes, questions or suggestions. We will start with a short video of product introduction, and the prototypes will be presented to you.

歡迎，請往這邊走。這是有關新產品的調查問卷。你也可以用它來寫下你的筆記、問題或建議。我們將從產品介紹的短片開始，再呈現樣品給您。

Possible answer 2

Ⓐ You are at the right place. Welcome to the focus group. Here is a notepad and a pen for you to write down your comments. I will take you to a meeting room with our product samples on the table. Feel free to touch and try on the backpack. And your response will become one of the factors to decide the price.

就是這裡，歡迎您蒞臨焦點小組。這裡有一本記事本和一支筆，可以讓您寫下您的意見。之後我會帶您到會議室，桌子有樣品。歡迎您隨意的觸摸和試用的背包樣品，且您的回應會成為決定這個背包售價的因素之一。

特助補給單字

facilitator *n.* 協調者

written *adj.* 書面

survey *n.* 民意調查

verbal *adj.* 口頭的

prototype *n.* 樣品

 秘書特助對答技巧提點

We have conducted a written survey prior to the focus group, and now we are looking forward to your verbal statement.

⊃ prior to 在……之前。例：A week prior to Paris fashion week, I have prepared 10 outfits and packed up all my accessories.（巴黎時裝週的前一個禮拜，我已經好準備好 10 套衣服，所有的配件也都打包好了。）

<u>Feel free to touch and try on the backpack.</u>

➲ Feel free to… 是常見的口語用法，代表「請隨意……」或是「請不要覺得有壓力……」。例 1：<u>Feel free to take a seat. The doctor will be right with you.</u>（請先找位子坐下，醫生馬上就為您看診。）例 2：<u>Feel free to contact me if you have any questions.</u>（如果有任何問題，請不吝指教。）

 秘書特助經驗分享

　　時尚業的市場調查除了常見的 SWOT 分析與焦點團體之外，還會包括國際刊物雜誌和網站、製造商的研發資訊、每年的流行色系、國際設計師觀點與意見，還有街頭流行報告等。時尚產業的發揮空間很大，如果你一向對數字很有概念，也許你可以考慮往市場調查這個方向發展喔！

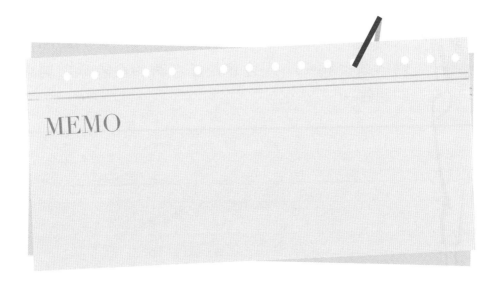

MEMO

秘書特助篇 ❶

秘書特助行銷公關篇 ❷

產品發表

Product release

 秘書特助工作內容介紹

　　每樣新產品都經過專業團隊長期的研發、測試、再經過包裝設計所產出的物件。新品創作的同時，相關的行銷策略與通路行銷也同時地在進行中。所投入的金錢與心血，就是期待新品發表（product launch）的那一刻。新品一上市就希望能造成討論，所以很多人會選擇舉辦新品發表會，邀請記者做媒體報導，或是針對目標群眾與部落客作新品介紹，盡量在最短時間內獲得最大的曝光，並在市場上產生影響力。你的新品活動話題性夠嗎？這將會是左右新品發表成功與否的關鍵。

職場上實況對談的一問二答　⊙ Track 27

新品發表會也需要設定清楚的目標，否則籌備的心力與行銷預算，也只會石沈大海。你追求的是媒體曝光、產品經銷、消費者的認知度或是產品銷量？你是想對舉辦展覽會、媒體記者會或是需要專業的評鑑與報導呢？定清楚目標後，你就可以開始擬 VIP 賓客邀請名單了。以下是特助 Amilia 與行銷團隊 Marketing 的問答：

Question 1

Ⓜ **We have reached an agreement on launching the new clothing line by hosting a fashion show to create consumer awareness; anyone wants to suggest a unique location for the event?**

我們之前已經決議要舉辦一場時裝秀來宣傳我們全新的服裝設計品牌，有人想提議特殊的活動場地嗎？

Possible answer 1

Ⓐ Normally, a fashion show is held in a stadium, a mall or a fancy hotel. Taking into considcration that our new brand represents nature and eco-friendly materials, I would like to propose that we hold the fashion show in a public garden.

通常服裝秀會選在體育館、百貨公司或是奢華的飯店裡舉行。考慮到我們的新品牌代表著自然和環保訴求，我想提議在公共的花園裡舉辦服裝秀。

Possible answer 2

Ⓐ Instead of one fashion show, I want to suggest that we break down the fashion show into several flash mob fashion shows. We can choose a long weekend and allow it to take place in different locations of fashion districts.

與其舉辦一個時裝秀，我想建議把時裝發表會分成幾個快閃時裝秀。我們可以選擇一個連假週末，在不同的鬧區舉辦快閃活動。

Question 2

Ⓜ **Our brand image has been reinvented when we hired a new designer last year, which greatly affected our brand image and style. We need to empower our brand image when we launch our new product line next season. Let's stay away from celebrity endorsements and focus on establishing a valuable brand, any ideas?**

我們去年聘請新的設計師之後，徹底顛覆了我們的品牌形象和風格。我們需要在下一季推出新產品線的時候，強化我們的品牌形象。如果我們不想要採用明星代言，對於建立一個有價值的品牌，你們有什麼想法嗎？

Possible answer 1

Ⓐ What about sponsoring a charitable cause? We can give back to the community while gaining a positive brand reputation. With the money we save on a product launch event, we can make a donation to an environmental organization; our customers can also participate in a good cause while making a purchase.

贊助慈善事業怎麼樣呢？在回饋社會的同時，也可以提升品牌聲譽。省下新品發表會的費用，我們可以捐贈給環境綠化組織，我們的客戶也可以透過購買，參與環保綠化做好事。

Possible answer 2

Ⓐ Our new brand is exploring the younger generation. I thought holding a design contest would attract a lot of attention among them. We can offer an appealing internship position as well as prize money and a chance to launch the contest winning designer piece.

我們的新品牌正在探索的年輕一代，我想舉辦設計大賽將吸引很多的年輕人的關注。我們可以提供一個有吸引力的實習職位，以及獎金和大賽獲獎設計師作品推出的機會。

特助補給單字

eco-friendly *adj.* 環保的

approachable *adj.* 平易近人的

aspiring *adj.* 有抱負的

秘書特助對答技巧提點

We have reached an agreement on launching the new clothing line by hosting a fashion show to create consumer awareness.

➲ Reach an agreement on＋N：在某個議題上達成協議。例 1：I am glad we have reached an agreement on the rental fee. I can't wait to move in here.（我很高興我們已經達成了租賃協議，我已經等不及要搬進來了。）例 2：We couldn't reach an agreement on the book title, so we have to reschedule for the next meeting in 2 weeks.（我們在書籍命名上無法達成協議，所以 2 週內還得再安排一次會議。）

Instead of one fashion show, I want to suggest that we break down the fashion show into several flash mob fashion shows.

➲ Instead of 取代、替代。例 1：Instead of going to the park, let's go get manicures.（與其去公園，我們改去做指甲吧！）例 2：He is allergic to seafood, so can we order chicken instead of fish?（他對海鮮過敏，所以我們可以不要點魚，改點雞肉嗎？）

秘書特助經驗分享

　　辦產品發表會的時候，地點的選擇幾乎是最重要的項目。交通不方便會大大地降低受邀者參加的意願。你希望來賓的心思花在欣賞新產品上，而不是為了找地點而傷腦筋。**Don't be afraid to think outside the box!** 只要場地與產品的性質不相抵觸，產品發表會應該要有意想不到的巧思，甚是以網路活動取代記者會，只要題材夠創新有趣，自然會吸引媒體報導。

❶ 秘書特助篇

❷ 秘書特助行銷公關篇

MEMO

記者會、開幕儀式

Press release and opening ceremony

秘書特助工作內容介紹

　　開記者會是發佈重要消息方式，目的是讓媒體幫助業主把消息傳達出去，藉以接觸更多更廣的群眾。新聞稿只能傳達消息，而記者會提供了與記者互動的機會。記者會有時候是用來澄清誤解，或是為了負面新聞止血，這時候對於社會的指控才有解釋的管道。對企業形象來說是絕對必要的。與記者直接面對面，你可以完整地介紹你的成果與對社會的正面影響。記者會如果辦得成功，還有可能出現在電視報導上，這所帶來的宣傳效果就是開記者會最理想的結果。

職場上實況對談的一問二答　 Track 28

記者會與開幕儀式，通常是為了要向社會大眾介紹新品牌、新公司或是重大消息的發佈。有時候也會為了特定目的召開閃電型的記者會，比方說讓競爭對手措手不及，或是針對某些社會議題突發性的發言，甚至對媒體也只在記者會招開前幾小時通知。以下是 Amilia 與記者 Beth:B 之間的問答：

Question 1

B Hey, Amilia. What a pleasant surprise! I thought I would see you here. Are you going to the fashion 2.0 meetups next week?

嗨，愛蜜莉亞，在這裡看到妳真是個驚喜！我才在想我會不會在這裡碰到妳呢！下禮拜時尚 **2.0** 的記者會妳會去嗎？

Possible answer 1

A Hello, Beth. Yes, I am. I am looking forward to it. This will be the first time I attend the event, where I get to meet fashion bloggers, tastemakers, media publishers and other fashion PR representatives. This is the perfect opportunity for networking and making new friends.

您好，貝絲，我會去參加喔！我非常的期待。這會是我第一次參加這個活動，在那裡我可以認識很多時尚部落客、潮流創造者、媒體出版商還有其他公司的時尚公關代表。這個活動是累積人脈和結交新朋友的好機會！

Possible answer 2

Ⓐ Yes, I go to the event every year! At this event, you get to meet all the famous and popular people in the fashion industry. Fashion 2.0 hosts the amazing press conference for online trendsetters whether you are a newbie in the industry or an industry insider. This is the event of the year you absolutely cannot miss.

當然，我每年都一定會去參加！在這個活動裡，你可以認識所有時尚界的名流。不管你是資深的時尚人或是剛入行的新手，由時尚 2.0 為數位時尚世界所舉辦的記者餐敘，絕對是你不能錯過的年度盛會。

Question 2

Ⓑ **Hi, Amilia. Thanks for the e-mail and the personal phone call to make sure that I got the message about the press conference. I will definitely be there, but do you think it's possible to give us a bit more information about the news?**

嗨！愛蜜莉亞，感謝您的電子郵件，還特地打電話過來，以確保我有收到記者會的召開通知。那天我一定會到，但妳可以稍微透露一點消息給我們嗎？

Possible answer 1

Ⓐ Thank you, Beth. It's the least I can do to make sure important media like you will attend our press conference. I don't wish to spoil the news but I highly suggest that you bring your camera crew with you.

謝謝您，貝絲，這是我該做的，以確保像您這樣的重要媒體，可以蒞臨我們的記者會。我不想破壞大家的驚喜，但我很建議你帶著你的攝影團隊。

Possible answer 2

Ⓐ I am so glad to hear that. We have crucial evidence that the accusation against our corporation is untrue. One of the politicians in our district will be a participant in our press conference, as well as our corporate lawyers. We are ready for all the questions that you may have.

我很高興您能參與我們的記者會。對於我們公司的不實指控，我們掌握至關重要的證據。除了我們社區的某政治人物會參與記者會之外，我們公司的律師團隊也會一同出席。對於媒體可能會有的問題，我們都有了萬全的準備。

秘書特助篇 ❶

秘書特助行銷公關篇 ❷

| 特助補給單字 |

tastemaker *n.* 風格開創者

publisher *n.* 出版商

accusation *n.* 指控

 秘書特助對答技巧提點

I don't wish to spoil the news but I highly suggest that you bring your camera crew with you.

⊃ Spoil 搞砸、損壞。例 1：Don't spoil the ending for me; I haven't finished watching this movie!（不要透露結局毀了我的興致，我還沒看完這部電影呢！）例 2：The party was spoiled after 3 times of police raid.（被警方搜查了 3 次之後，這個派對也結束了。）

We have crucial evidence that the accusation against our corporation is untrue.

⊃ Against 介系詞，指反對、違反。例 1：I have nothing against you, but I think with your profession, you will be much happier in retail instead of merchandising.（我對你沒有任何偏見，但考慮到你的專業，我想你在零售部會更快樂，而不是留在商品採購。）例 2：Try not to hold a grudge against each other and be open for a discussion.（盡量不要互相怨恨，並且考慮敞開心房進行討論。）

秘書特助經驗分享

　　記者會有幾個不成文的規定，比方說儘量避開週一和週五。原因是週一通常是最忙碌的一天，而週五則是因為隔天就是週末，媒體會來不及撰寫新聞。再來，記者會最好舉辦在早上 10 點到 11 點間，這樣還有機會可以在下午或晚間上新聞。開記者會的時候，不需要期待所有的媒體都能出現，畢竟當天發生的事件都有可能成為你的競爭對手。

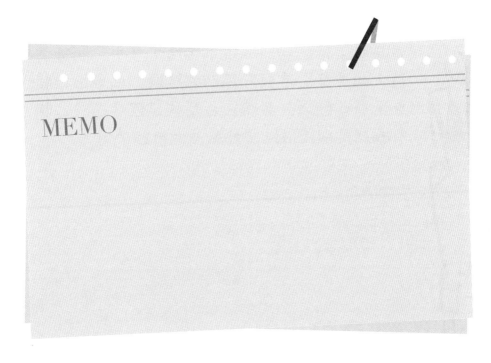

MEMO

UNIT 5　國外廠商招待與關係維持

Receiving and networking with foreign suppliers

 秘書特助工作內容介紹

　　以歐洲的時尚品牌來說，多數來自法國與義
大利。以經銷法國品牌的臺灣分公司或是代理商
為例，採購與公關每年至少得出差到法國兩次。
除了參與春夏與秋冬新品發表會可以立即下單採
購之外，參與國外廠商舉辦的活動、展現對品牌
的支持與熱情，才能建立長久互信的商業關係。
當品牌業務來亞洲巡視市場時，會由公關負責接
待，如果有需要對方協助的議題，也會由公關代
為溝通或翻譯。品牌在台灣的媒體曝光，公關也
有義務定期提供給國外廠商做行銷使用。

職場上實況對談的一問二答　 Track 29

出差到國外參與合作廠商的展覽，除了可以馬上挑出適合台灣市場的款式與質料之外，每年接觸國際時尚潮流與了解競爭廠商動向，也是維持時尚公關靈敏度的不二法則。以下是 Amilia 與義大利傢俱廠商 Carlotta 之間的問答：

Question 1

C Hi, Amilia. I am so glad you made it! I can't wait to show you the new furniture collection that we have. As you can see, polished surface and linen fabric are very happening this year. Did you want to check out dinning tables?

嗨，愛蜜莉亞，很高興看到妳來！我等不及要想向妳介紹新品。正如妳所看到的，拋光表面和亞麻織品今年非常熱門。妳是不是說過特別想看餐桌呢？

Possible answer 1

A Hello, Carlotta. It's so great to see you, too! Yes, you remembered. We have a very high demand for dining tables and dining chairs in Taiwan. The South African white granite oval dinning table was a best-seller last season. Now we want to add big round dining tables and armchairs into our showroom.

妳好，卡洛塔，我也好高興見到妳！沒錯，妳還記得，台灣市場對餐桌和餐椅的需求很多。上一季的南非白色花崗岩橢

圓形餐桌一直都很暢銷。現在我們想要添加大圓餐桌和扶手椅到我們的展示空間。

Possible answer 2

Ⓐ Hey, Carlotta. How are you doing? I am so excited about the new furniture! This polished metal side table is an eye opener. Yes, we are always looking for unique dining tables, sofas and coffee tables.

嗨，卡洛塔，妳好嗎？我很期待這次的新品家具！這種拋光金屬邊桌真的很搶眼。是的，我們一直在尋找獨特的餐桌、沙發和咖啡桌。

Question 2

Ⓒ **Hi, Amilia. I got up earlier than usual because of jetlag. Do you mind if we meet in the showroom now instead of this afternoon?**

嗨，愛蜜莉亞，因為時差，我太早起床了。你介意我們下午在展示間的會面，提前到現在嗎？

Possible answer 1

Ⓐ Not at all. Please come in. As you can see, we mix and match different brands together to create a harmonious living space. We only select handcrafted natural materials, such as swamp wood coffee tables, bronze display shelves, mouth blown glass pendant lighting and granite dining tables. I think they really blend in with the sofa and the armchair from you.

當然不介意,歡迎您進來。正如你所看到的,我們混搭不同品牌,創造一個和諧的生活空間。我們只選擇手工製作的天然素材,例如沼澤樹咖啡桌、青銅陳列架、口吹玻璃吊具和花崗岩餐桌。我覺得他們和妳們的沙發和扶手椅很相配。

Possible answer 2

🅐 By all means. Our showroom is always open to you. We just finished rearranging the space because all the new items from you came in last week. I am looking forward to your opinions and discussing a new project about a luxury apartment in Taipei.

當然可以,我們的展示空間永遠歡迎妳。因為上週妳們的新品到貨了,我們就重新佈置了空間。我想聽聽妳的看法,並一起討論台北豪華公寓的專案。

特助補給單字

oval *adj.* 橢圓形

jetlag *n.* 時差

harmonious *adj.* 協調的

秘書特助對答技巧提點

We have a very high demand for dining tables and dining chairs in Taiwan.

➲ demand for something 對某個事物有需求／需要。high demand vs. low demand 高度需求 vs. 需求不高。例 1：There is a high demand for clean food and water in Africa.（目前非洲很需要乾淨的食物和水。）

例 2：In our job market today, the demand for higher education has dropped during the past 5 years.（在今天的就業市場上，對高等教育的需求在過去 5 年中有所下降。）

I think they really blend in with the sofa and the armchair from you.

➲ Blend 原先是混合的意思，而 blend in 就有融為一體的意思，後面接受詞可用 with 這個介系詞，成為 blend in with「與……調和」的用法。

例 1：She cut her hair short to join the basketball team so she can blend in.（為了參加籃球隊她把頭髮剪短了，好讓她跟大家可以融為一體。）

例 2：She really blends in with the culture by drinking sake and wearing kimono in Japan.（她在日本喝清酒也穿和服，的確是入境隨俗。）

秘書特助經驗分享

　　與國外廠商相處的時候，台灣人好客的心態容易太過於禮貌。歐美供應商重視的並非是你送了多少伴手禮，或是請他吃大餐。重點還是要放在每年進貨的數量與品牌形象的維持。當你在招待對方的時候，只要注重禮貌與商業道德、培養互相尊重與信賴的關係，才是長久合作的關鍵所在。

MEMO

秘書特助工作內容介紹

記者會、開幕典禮或是公司對外活動都需要媒體接待。事前的準備工作有媒體資料（press kit）的撰寫，內容包含公司介紹（bio）、針對記者會主題的新聞稿（press release）和問題回答（Q&A）。Press kit 是為了方便媒體發佈新聞的時候，手邊就有足夠的文字內容與圖片可供使用，這樣可以大幅提升消息得到曝光的機會。一個稱職的媒體公關（publicist）除了會做好事前的資料準備、媒體名單的掌握，也會事先到會場確定一切硬體與軟體設備的運作正常，這樣媒體接待的準備工作就完成囉！

職場上實況對談的一問二答　 Track 30

媒體接待除了將場地準備完備，與來賓親自打招呼更是重要，維護彼此之間的良好互動，能讓企業訊息的能見度更高。另外在會場的招待處，要有專人記錄下媒體的聯絡方式，這對日後辦活動與新聞稿的發送也會很有幫助喔！以下是 Amilia 與行銷部 Marketing 和媒體 Reporter 互動之間的問答：

Question 1

Ⓜ**Hi, Amilia. Not all of our marketing team members are experienced in meeting with the media. Do you think you can give them some advice about how to polish their public relations skills?**

嗨！愛蜜莉亞，我們行銷團隊的成員，並不是每個人都有和媒體接觸的經驗，對於增強公關技能，妳願意給他們幾個建議嗎？

Possible answer 1

ⒶI would love to! Public relations is a profession dealing with media and important customers. You need to be attentive to details and be a critical thinker. You need to be able to communicate your thoughts accurately, as well as be a good listener.

我很樂意！公共關係是面對媒體和重要的客戶的一門專業，你需要注重細節，擁有評論的能力。你必須要準確傳達你的

想法，同時也得扮演良好的傾聽者。

Possible answer 2

🅰 I will be more than happy to talk to you about public relation skills! First of all, you need to work on your writing ability. Media receive numerous news releases every day. Only mesmerizing content will capture their attention. Writing articles on your personal blog is a good way to practice.

我會很樂意跟大家討論公關技巧！首先你需要加強你的寫作能力。媒體每天都會收到很多新聞稿，你需要打動人心的內容才能吸引他們的注意力。在你的個人部落格發表文章也是練習的好辦法。

Question 2

🆁 Hi, I am Ann from Taipei Daily News; I got an invitation from Amilia for the new product release press conference?

妳好！我是台北每日新聞的記者，安。愛蜜莉亞發了新品發表會的邀請函給我？

Possible answer 1

🅰 It's a pleasure to meet you, Ann. I am Amilia. Thank you so much for coming. The press conference will start in 10 minutes. We have refreshments prepared for you here, and here is a USB flash drive with a press kit and all the other information you will need about our new product. Would you be so kind and sign in here?

安，很高興認識您，我是愛蜜莉亞，非常感謝您的參與。新品發表會將在 10 分鐘內開始。我們有為您準備了茶點，這個是含有新聞稿資料的隨身碟，所有您需要的產品訊息都在裡面了。可以麻煩您在這裡簽名嗎？

Possible answer 2

Ⓐ Hello, I am Amilia. Welcome to our new product release conference! Here is a copy of the press kit and we have a photo booth here today, as well as our newly released photo frame as a gift. Please take a photo and upload it on Instagram or Facebook, and the person that gets the most "likes" will receive a gift set that's valued up to 300 dollars. Please enjoy the champagne and the presentation that's about to take place.

您好，我就是愛蜜莉亞，歡迎來到我們的新品發佈會！這份是新聞稿，我們今天準備了一個照相區，還有這是新品相框小禮物。請和它拍照並上傳到 Instagram 或臉書的照片，得到最多迴響的人將可獲贈一套價值 300 美元的精美禮品。請享受我們準備的香檳和即將開始的新品介紹吧！

> 特助補給單字

attentive *adj.* 留意的

numerous *adj.* 許多的

mesmerizing *adj.* 迷人的

refreshment *n.* 茶點

upload *v.* 上傳

 秘書特助對答技巧提點

Not all of our marketing team members are experienced in meeting with media. Do you think you can give them some advice about how to polish their public relation skills?

➲ Be experienced in＋Ving 經歷過某件事，或對某件事很熟悉。例 1：I am experienced in installing pendant lights and other electric appliances in the house.（我對於安裝吊燈和其他居家電器非常有經驗。）例 2：She is not experienced in speaking in public, so she has been practicing for days.（她幾乎沒有公開演說的經歷，所以她已經練習了好幾天。）

➲ Polish 潤飾、精煉，通常用來表達把某種技能訓練得更專精。例 1：I will need to polish my Japanese because I haven't spoken it for years.（我需要好好練習我的的日

文，因為我已經很多年沒説過日文了。）例 2：We spent weeks on <u>polishing</u> the corporate message, now it's finally ready to be online.（我們花了好幾個禮拜潤飾企業訊息，現在終於準備好可以上傳官網了。）

 秘書特助經驗分享

　　一個時尚公關除了應有的溝通技巧與專業技能之外，擁有創意會讓你的工作更出色。創意除了豐富你的新聞稿內容，辦活動與記者會也會更有話題性。身為一個公關代表，你必須掌握所有最新的資訊，並應用在提升公司形象與品牌能見度上。這也是維持創意來源的方法之一喔！

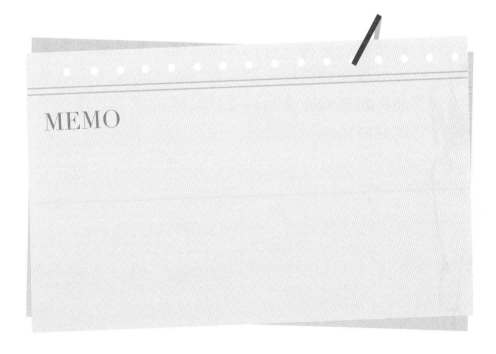

MEMO

平面媒體版面爭取與內容溝通
Obtaining print media exposure and content communication

 秘書特助工作內容介紹

公關與媒體之間的關係，是相輔相成的。公關舉辦專訪、記者會、提供精彩的產品內容，與產業最新的資訊給媒體報導，亦或是經常性的採購廣告版面，媒體也會回饋免費的產品曝光給品牌公關。公關每個月都應該主動與媒體接觸，經常性提供新品新聞稿，或是符合雜誌報導的主題商品。保持友好的溝通管道，當有新消息需要多加曝光的時候，通常都能派上用場。當展示空間有新品或是重新佈置的時候，就是約媒體午茶的好時機！

職場上實況對談的一問二答 Track 31

與媒體交流的時候，不需要太過嚴謹，可以把對方當成好朋友寒暄，讓互動盡量自然、熱絡。開心聊天之餘，再把新品或品牌消息傳達給對方。新聞稿內容一定要簡潔有力，讓對方無後顧之憂地寫稿，也會增加對方願意與你合作的意願。以下是 Amilia 與雜誌媒體 Layla 的問答：

Question 1

L Hey, Amilia. I've got your monthly newsletter. Thank you so much. Next month is Lunar New Year, so we are collecting new products in red and gold colors that represent good fortune. Do you have products that you would recommend our readers for home décor ideas?

嗨！愛蜜莉亞，我收到妳這個月的訊息了，謝謝妳。下個月就是春節，所以我們正在蒐集代表好運的紅色和金色的新產品。妳那裡有什麼產品可以推薦我們讀者，作為家居裝飾的建議嗎？

Possible answer 1

A The pleasure is all mine! We have just had the perfect item for home décor ideas during Lunar New Year. Our New armchair collection called Miranda is a vintage Italian design that's made from the finest fabric. The stylish velvet red color will light up any room in the house; it's the perfect addition in the most important holiday of the year.

我非常樂意！我這邊有很適合農曆新年期間的家居飾品。米蘭達扶手椅採用了最頂級的布料，是復古意大利的設計風格。時髦的的紅色天鵝絨能點亮家裡的任何角落，一年中最重要的節日了絕對少不了它。

Possible answer 2

Ⓐ You are welcome and thank you for always helping us with brand media exposure. Lunar New Year is when everyone gathers at the house and enjoys quality time together. Our bar chair Olivia might be a fun addition to your home. You can choose up to 200 fabrics, and of course it comes in beautiful red and gold colored fabrics that would provide your house with elegance and comfort.

不客氣，感謝您總是大力幫助我們作品牌曝光。農曆新年是和家人相聚，享受美好時光的時刻，我們的奧利維亞高腳椅，可以為您的家中做點變化。有多達 200 種花色可供選擇，當然也有美麗的紅色和金色的布料，提供優雅和舒適的居家環境。

Question 2

Ⓛ Hello, Amilia. I would like to invite you to a party! In 2 weeks, we are holding an interior

designer award. We are giving awards to innovative designers. You should come down here to have a good time and meet interior designers. Are you going to be free on the 25ᵗʰ?

嗨！愛蜜莉亞，我想邀請妳參加一個聚會！2 週內我們要舉辦室內設計師頒獎活動，把獎項送給創新的室內設計師。你應該過來看看，順便認識一些室內設計師，你 25 號有空嗎？

Possible answer 1

Ⓐ Hey, Layla. It's so good to hear from you. I would never miss the party. The annual interior design award is a great place for networking because all the best interior designers in the industry will be there.

嗨，萊拉，聽到妳的聲音真開心。我絕不會錯過這個盛會。一年一度的室內設計頒獎典禮是經營人脈的好機會，因為業界最好的室內設計師都會在這裡出現。

Possible answer 2

Ⓐ Hello, Layla. The interior design award is finally here! Of course, I will be there. Do you mind if I bring our sales manager along to the party? He is very experienced in luxury furniture and accessories.

您好，萊拉，室內設計大獎的時候又到了！我當然會參加。

你介意我帶我們的業務經理一起參加嗎？他在精品傢俱傢飾業有很豐富的經歷。

特助補給單字

lunar *adj.* 農曆的

fortune *n.* 福氣

award *n.* 獎項

innovative *adj.* 創新的

 秘書特助對答技巧提點

I've got your monthly newsletter. Thank you so much.

⊃ Monthly newsletter 每月新聞稿。Monthly 是時間副詞，許多業界的訊息都是每月更新，所以 monthly 可以和很多名詞合用。比方説：

monthly subscription 每月訂閱（可以是新聞稿、雜誌或是產業訊息）或 monthly review 每月評論。例：I see her once in a while at the monthly marketing meeting.（我和她偶爾會在行銷部月會碰到面。）

The stylish velvet red color will light up any room in the house.

⟳ Light up 點亮。例 1：Her smile lights up the room.（她的微笑點亮了這個小房間。）例 2：Her witty comment light up the hectic business conference.（她詼諧的評論，讓繁瑣的商務會議出現一線生機。）

You can choose up to 200 fabrics, and of course it comes in beautiful red and gold colored fabrics that would provide your house with elegance and comfort.

⟳ Up to... 是用來量化數字或是時間，是「最多為……」、「至多為……」的意思。例 1：This voucher can be deducted for a personal trainer session up to 2 hours.（這張優惠券最多可折抵 2 小時的私人健身教練課程。）例 2：You can choose up to 5 different side dishes with the set menu option.（加點附餐選項，您可以選擇多達 5 種不同的配菜。）

 秘書特助經驗分享

　　公關除了要主動出擊聯繫媒體，當媒體有派對邀請，或是活動協助的邀約，能夠積極配合當然是最好的。當媒體辦活動的時候，也希望參與人數多，氣氛熱鬧。如果你經常拒絕，不但以後不會收到邀請函，媒體也會不想報導你們的品牌消息。

人物專訪
Exclusive interviews

 秘書特助工作內容介紹

　　時尚的世界總是令人嚮往，所以時尚界大人物的專訪，很容易引起關注。身為時尚界的行銷公關，你很有可能需要專訪自家的設計師或是總裁，提供給媒體作題材。如果你是時尚編輯，你作專訪的機會就更多了。多彩多姿的人生故事與心路歷程，一直到最後成功的祕訣，可以鼓舞成千上萬擁有時尚夢的後輩們。你也可以透過人物專訪，得到許多業界裡的寶貴經驗與獨特見解。能夠貼近這些時尚界的佼佼者，與他們交換意見，也能夠幫助你實現自己的時尚理想喔！

職場上實況對談的一問二答　　◉ Track 32

時尚業的美感來源，絕對不止是時尚限定的題材。有可能來自建築、夢境或是設計師的成長環境等等。透過人物專訪，可以洞悉一個品牌的靈魂精神與設計師的設計概念，品牌也能透過人物專訪，為品牌形象加分。以下是公關 Amilia 與設計師 Phoebe 專訪的問答內容：

Question 1

P **Amilia, thank you for meeting me in my studio today. I can give you a tour if that helps with the interview. Can I get you anything before we start?**

愛蜜莉亞，謝謝你願意過來我的工作室會面。如果對採訪有幫助，我也可以帶你看看環境。在我們開始之前，我可以幫你準備點什麼嗎？

Possible answer 1

A Thanks, Phoebe. I am good. I would like to take this opportunity to show our appreciation; our fans are so excited about this interview. I have collected a few of the most frequently-asked-questions from our fan page, and the first one is when you decided to start a career in the fashion industry, and why you chose to work with Mexican textiles.

謝謝你，菲比，我現在不需要。我想藉這次的機會表達我們對你的感激。我們的粉絲很期待這次的專訪。我從粉絲頁收

集了最常被問到的問題，第一個是你什麼時候決定進入時尚行業，還有為什麼會選擇墨西哥紡織來創作？

Possible answer 2

A A cup of coffee would be nice, thank you. I have always admired your work since your first collection; I am your biggest fan. We would really like to know where you studied to become a fashion artist since there are so many people who want to follow in your footsteps.

一杯咖啡就好了，謝謝你。我很喜歡你的作品，從你第一個系列開始，我就是你最忠實的粉絲。我們想知道你在哪裡學習，而成為時尚藝術家，因為有很多人，想要跟隨您的腳步。

Question 2

P I never went to an art school, and I wanted to be a writer. So I took a part time in the textile company to support my writing career. That's when I found my calling. You never know where life can take you. Did that answer your question?

我從未進入藝術學校學習，我本來想成為一個作家。所以去紡織公司兼職，以支持我的寫作生涯，然後在那邊發現我這一生的志業。你永遠不知道人生會帶你往哪裡去。這算回答了你的問題嗎？

Possible answer 1

Ⓐ Yes, I think that will encourage a lot of people that are looking for a career change. Could you kindly tell us the biggest lesson you have learned from starting your own label, and are there any suggestions that you would give young designers who are about to start a new brand?

是的，我認為這會鼓勵很多在考慮轉換跑道的人。你在創立您的品牌之後，學到最大的教訓是什麼？另外，你會給即將要創立新品牌的年輕設計師什麼建議？

Possible answer 2

Ⓐ Yes, being a self-taught artist is certainly adding a twist in your fascinating career. Your career is exactly like your clothing, rich and complicated. About personal style, what is your favorite accessory? And what is the one thing that you will never wear?

是的，作為一個自學成才的藝術家，肯定在你令人著迷的職業生涯添加了轉折。您的事業就像您的衣著，豐富而複雜。關於個人的風格，您最喜歡的配件是什麼？您絕對不會穿的衣服又是什麼呢？

特助補給單字

studio *n.* 工作室

admire *v.* 仰慕

textile *n.* 布料

label *n.* 商標

twist *n.* 轉折

 秘書特助對答技巧提點

Can I get you anything before we start?

➜ 這句話通常出現在去拜訪客戶，或是拜訪某個人家的時候，對方的禮貌問候。大致的意思是，你需要點什麼嗎？這句話可以泛指，你肚子餓嗎？需要喝水嗎？想要吃點甜點嗎？也可以用「Can I get you anything?」來取代。例：Can I get you anything? No, thanks.（我可以為您做什麼嗎？不用了，謝謝。）

I would like to take this opportunity to show our appreciation.

➜ I would like to take this opportunity to... 我希望藉由這個機會來……。這是一個很常見的句型，你可以套用在很多不同狀況裡。例 1：I would like to take this opportunity to say a few words.（我想趁今天這個機會跟大家說幾句

話。）例 2：I would like to take this opportunity to apologize for my behavior last time.（我希望藉由這個機會，為我上次的行為道歉。）

Yes, being a self taught artist is certainly adding a twist in your fascinating career.

つ Self-taught 自學的；未受過正式教育或課程。例：She is a self-taught vocalist and sings twice a week at a popular club.（她是一位自學的歌手，每星期 2 天都會在一個很受歡迎的夜店駐唱。）

 秘書特助經驗分享

　　個人專訪除了一些背景經驗，你也可以詢問對方未來的規劃。比方說接下來五年的人生目標，或是接下來十年的品牌走向。你也可以問一些比較有趣的問題，例如是否有宗教信仰、特殊的飲食習慣、害怕的東西是什麼？這些小問題可以讓大牌設計師顯得人性化，也可以提升品牌親和力喔！

展覽申請與企劃
Exhibition application and planning

 秘書特助工作內容介紹

　　參加展覽是展示新品的方式之一，對於時尚業來說，如果沒有把設計的款式推廣出去，等於無法有營收利潤與發展空間。參與大型展覽的好處是同業聚集，自然人潮多，曝光率也高。但全面對外開放，難免會無形中把資源消耗在非主訴求的客群上，因此參與大型展覽並不適用於所有時尚品牌。展覽的申請與展場的設計規劃，是全公司對外展示的品牌形象，必須由專業的公關人才來把關。展覽期間的人力配置，打造舒適方便的展覽空間亦是公關的職責之一。

職場上實況對談的一問二答 Track 33

國內外有許多大型展覽，時尚界還多了歐美的時尚週，時尚週前後還有其他展出的機會，總是吸引了全世界各地的時尚採購。參展前你得先瞭解市場，你希望設計的產品可以突出，但不至於太過前衛而無法被市場接受。以下是 Amilia 與展覽單位 Exhibit 之間的問答。

Question 1

E **Hi, Amilia. We got your application inquiry about the fall fashion exhibit. I would like to inform you that you are qualified to apply for an unit. An application form has already been sent to your e-mail account. Please let me know if you have any further questions. We will be happy to assist you.**

您好，愛蜜莉亞，我們已經收到您提出參加秋季時裝展您的詢問信件。貴公司已經獲得資格可以申請一個單位，申請表已經同時發送到您的電子信箱了。如果您有任何問題，請讓我知道，我們將竭誠為您服務。

Possible answer 1

A Thank you so much for the prompt reply. I do have a few questions that I would like to ask you. Could you advise us which gallery should we apply to for a large-scale fashion outfit exhibit?

非常感謝您的及時答覆。我的確有幾個問題想請教您。如果我們想舉辦大型時裝展覽，請問我們該申請哪個會場會比較適合呢？

Possible answer 2

Ⓐ Thank you for the great news. We are very excited about holding our first wedding dress collection exhibit in your fall fashion exhibit. Would you suggest that we hold the dress exhibit in the main gallery? We really like how it has a sunroof and a semi stage; we have some great ideas about decorating it into an autumn dream wedding.

謝謝您帶來的好消息，對於即將在秋季時裝展覽舉行我們的第一次的婚紗個展，我們感到非常興奮。您會建議我們在主要會場展覽我們的禮服嗎？我們真的很喜歡那個場地的天窗和小舞台。我們有一些不錯的點子，想把它裝飾成一個秋天的夢幻婚禮。

Question 2

Ⓔ **Hello, Amila. After a careful consideration of your exhibit application, we think with the scale of your accessory collection, we suggest that you apply for our Jewel Gallery, which is more economical and suitable for exhibiting delicate art pieces. Please don't hesitate if you have any**

questions.

您好，愛蜜莉亞，針對您提出的參展申請，經過慎重考慮後，我們認為以貴公司的展覽規模，建議您可以申請我們的珠寶展覽會場。這樣不但更經濟，也比較適合展演精緻的小型藝術品。如果您有任何疑問，請不要猶豫，歡迎您的詢問。

Possible answer 1

Ⓐ Thank you for the great advice! We are going to take your word for it. Although the main hall's got a beautiful high ceiling, with our rings and hairpin collection, the Jewel Gallery does seem to be more approachable and personal.

謝謝您寶貴的意見！我們決定採用您的建議了。雖然大會堂有漂亮的挑高天花板，但如果用來展示我們的戒指和髮夾，珠寶會場似乎更較具有親和力和個人風格。

Possible answer 2

Ⓐ Thank you for the professional advice. I will definitely consider the Jewel Gallery. Apart from the actual collection, we also have a 10 minute "in the making" and the design concept video that we would like to display. We can bring in our own equipment. Could you advice if that's possible?

謝謝你的專業見解，我們肯定會將珠寶藝廊列入考慮。除了我們展示的物件之外，我們還準備了 10 分鐘的「製作過

程」和設計理念的企業影片，想一併作展示。我們可以帶自
己的設備過去，請問這樣有可行性嗎？

特助補給單字

prompt *adj.* 及時的

sunroof *n.* 天窗

hesitate *v.* 猶豫

ceiling *n.* 天花板

 秘書特助對答技巧提點

We got your application inquiry about the fall fashion
exhibit. I would like to inform you that you are qualified to
apply for an unit.

- Inquiry 詢問。商業書信中很常會提到這個單字，用來詢問商
  品資訊或產品價格。例：I got an inquiry about our
  wholesale price for the carpet and minimum
  requirement.（我收到一封詢問地毯批發價格和最低訂量的
  信件。）

- Be qualified to V 指到達做某事的資格。例：My husband
  was qualified to apply for upper management
  positions.（我先生符合資格可以申請高層管理職位。）

We also have a 10 minute "in the making" and the design concept video that we would like to display.

⊃ In the making 主要是要詮釋 making 這個動作，通常是工藝過程的呈現，或是影片幕後花絮等等製作過程的呈現。例：
This film was six years <u>in the making</u>, and it turned out to be a huge success.（這部電影經過長達六年的製作期，最後成為曠世巨作。）

秘書特助經驗分享

申請展覽資格的時候，除了參展的作品之外，還有很多文件要交附喔！例如展覽企劃、展覽主題、設計師履歷和作品圖片。辦展期間的交通建議要事先確認，有的大型展覽週邊會有交通管制，展覽的期間所有車輛都是禁止通行喔！另外如果你的展示品十分貴重，你可以考慮加買保險，以免展期間有可能有汙損、破壞或是竊盜等問題。

品牌核心掌握與品牌建立

Buidling brand image and corporate core values

秘書特助工作內容介紹

　　一個企業的成功，除了要有優秀的員工、好的商品與行銷策略之外，品牌的建立更是關乎公司是否能永續經營的重點。一個優秀的公關人才，會懂得如何找出品牌優勢，並運用所有資源來推動品牌在市場上的能見度與影響力（You need to create a strong brand for your company, find out their distinctive features and promote them with your resources.）。一個時尚品牌，必須要在消費者心中有顯著的風格和形象，才算是成功的品牌經營。公關要有凝聚品牌形象的能力，也要瞭解你所經營的目標群眾具備的特性，你的行銷預算就能花在刀口上。

職場上實況對談的一問二答　 Track 34

公關可以說是品牌背後的操刀手，品牌要在市場上顯而易見，勢必為公關幕後的努力推動與宣傳。一個企業的經營理念，也會需要由公關不斷地透過方式對外傳達，市場對於品牌才會有正確的概念以下是 Amilia 與行銷部 Marketing 和編輯 Editor 之間的問答：

Question 1

Ⓜ **Thank you for sharing your insights into the brand strategy with us today. Brand building in the fashion industry can be so exciting yet frustrating, so we are really eager to hear from you today!**

感謝您今天與我們分享品牌戰略方面的見解，在時尚界建立品牌可以是精彩，卻又令人沮喪的過程，所以真的很期待您的演說！

Possible answer 1

Ⓐ Thank you for inviting me to speak at this brand strategy workshop. I am happy to share my experiences in the industry with you. What is a brand? It's the hopes and dreams that a product or a service can provide you. First of all, you need to define your best-selling point, then you can decide how you would like to express the story.

謝謝您邀請我來品牌戰略研討會演講，我很樂意與大家分享我在時尚業的經驗。什麼是品牌？品牌就是一個產品或服務能夠提供給你希望和夢想。首先你需要找出最大的賣點，接下來你就可以決定用什麼樣的方式來表達你的故事。

Possible answer 2

Ⓐ It's an honor to be here among marketing experts and top salesmen. To successfully promote your brand, you need to carefully consider the core value of your brand. In another word, what is the personality of your brand?

能面對這麼多行銷專家和超級業務是我的榮幸。為了成功地推廣自己的品牌，你需要仔細考慮你品牌的核心價值。換句話說，品牌的特性是什麼？核心精神是什麼？能區隔你和你的競爭對手的又是什麼？而最重要的是，公司內部所有的員工都必須先了解品牌的故事。

Question 2

Ⓔ Your select shop has covered quite a lot of collections from different fashion brands and it's been a huge hit with the market. How did it all start?

您的複合式店舖涵蓋了非常多不同的時尚品牌，且已在市場上產生不小的衝擊。您可以告訴我們這一切是怎麼開始的嗎？

Possible answer 1

🅐 Being a fashion consumer, we understand how difficult it is to find great products with unique designs that are full of details in one stop. That's why we decided to open our select shop.

作為一個時尚重度消費者，我們理解在同一家店，找齊擁有獨特設計又充滿細節的商品是多麼困難的一件事。這就是為什麼我們決定成立我們的複合式商店。

Possible answer 2

🅐 We understand having an outfit everyday isn't an easy task. So our select shop takes your measurements and delivers a new outfit to your doorstep monthly. We have a great relationship with our suppliers and our customers who help us deliver the best shopping experience in the industry.

我們理解每天都擁有完整的服裝配件穿搭很不容易。因此我們的複合式商店會測量您的尺寸，每個月準備一整套服裝送到您家門口。我們與供應商和客戶的關係良好，他們幫助我們提供業界最佳的購物體驗。

▌特助補給單字

workshop *n.* 工作室

define *v.* 下定義

doorstep *n.* 門口

秘書特助對答技巧提點

First of all, you need to define your best-selling point, then you can decide how you would like to express the story.

➲ Best-selling point 最大的賣點。例 1：The best-selling point of the movie is that main character, not the plot.
（這部影片的最佳賣點是主角，而不是情節。）例 2：Our handcraftsmanship is our best-selling point. Without saying, comfort and quality are prerequisites of our brand.（我們的手工編織工藝是最大的賣點，當然，舒適性和質感是我們的品牌的必要條件。）

We have a great relationship with our suppliers and our customers who help us deliver the best shopping experience in the industry.

➲ Deliver 一般來說是運送、傳遞的意思。但在文中的用法則是「實現」的意思。例：With the support from our team and funders, we were able to deliver our dream of creating an animal welfare foundation.（在我們的團隊和資助者的支持之下，我們才能實現我們成立動物福利基金會的夢想。）

秘書特助經驗分享

　　許多品牌的成功來自於他們提供了客戶更好的生活品質，在建立品牌的時候，你的服務是否解決了消費者的問題？會讓他願意再次消費嗎？每一個環節，都替消費者細心着想，讓購物過程方便。很多消費者會願意把好的服務推薦出去，這樣口碑行銷的慢慢累積，會比廣告行銷來得更感動人心。

❶ 秘書特助篇

❷ 秘書特助行銷公關篇

MEMO

品牌介紹與品牌形象維持
Brand introduction and corporate image maintenance

 秘書特助工作內容介紹

　　作為一個時尚精品業的公關，你的談吐與內涵，你發出去的每一封新聞稿、信件或是對外發言，都代表著公司形象。基本上除了消費者端，公關有職責接待國外供應商、媒體、雜誌編輯、同業廠商，以及其它相關採購企業的聯絡窗口。溝通協調的手腕要好，良好的語言能力，通常也是成為企業公關的必備條件之一。經常要對外介紹公司的你，對於公司的歷史發展、品牌設計精神、設計師背景與產品的特色，都得滾瓜爛熟。當你真心喜歡自家品牌，推薦品牌將會更有說服力。

職場上實況對談的一問二答　　　◉ Track 35

時尚精品通常會有美輪美奐的展示空間（showroom），定期有新品替換陳列，與陳列空間的更新、佈置。這樣一來，客戶才會知道需要定期回顧，才不會錯失好東西。而公關也會在新品上市的時候，邀請媒體或編輯來 showroom 參觀新品，爭取產品曝光的機會。以下是 Amelia 與雜誌編輯 Nick 的問答：

Question 1

Ⓝ **Hey, Amilia. Thank you for sponsoring the trip to the leather factory in Italy. It really allows us to report an in-depth story in the fashion industry. Ever since the trip, I have been looking forward to fine leather goods for the new season because I witnessed the birth of a timeless design. Wow, am I looking at the It bag of 2016?**

嗨，愛蜜莉亞，謝謝你們贊助我們去義大利參觀皮革廠。讓我們能深入報導時裝界的精彩內幕。從那次的旅程之後，我一直期待著下一季的精品皮件，因為我見證了這經典設計的過程。哇，這是 **2016** 年最受矚目的包款嗎？

Possible answer 1

Ⓐ Good eye! It's called the Havana clutch, inspired by an exotic trip the designer took on the spur of the moment. The bag is made with a patchwork of grained leather and velvet with flap front clutch with metal pin embellishment.

好眼力！這是哈瓦那手拿包，設計概念來自於設計師臨時起意的一趟異國之旅。高檔皮革與天鵝絨的交錯設計，有金屬配件點綴與前扣開口的設計。

Possible answer 2

🅰 Yes, it is! The bucket bag was crafted from a supple textured leather with a wide wrist strap. The interior is spacious enough to carry an A4 size folder! For the spring collection, there is a limited edition of silver stud version. This bag was used in NY fashion week as the after party gift bag, loaded with goodies such as a Chanel eye pencil, Dior red lipstick and our spring line of hand cream.

沒錯！這個水桶包採用柔軟的皮革來製作，還有寬版的手腕提把。內部容量大，足以攜帶 A4 大小的文件夾！春夏款還有限量的銀製鉚釘設計。這個包被選為紐約時裝週會後派對的伴手禮，裡面裝了許多好東西，比方說香奈兒眼線筆、迪奧紅色唇膏和我們春季新款的護手霜。

Question 2

🅽 Hey, Amilia. I am impressed with the new wedding dress collection. Given that this is the first bridal campaign, which one would you say is the signature piece?

嗨！愛蜜莉亞，你們的婚紗款式很令人驚艷，考慮到這是你們第一次發表婚紗，哪一件你會說是經典之作呢？

Possible answer 1

Ⓐ Thank you so much for the compliment. It really means a lot coming from you. Well, each of our bridal dresses is very unique. For instance, this 2-piece wedding dress is our best-seller right now. The floor-sweeping lace skirt and the cropped top are perfect designs for an urban bride.

非常感謝您的讚美，這些話來自你更顯得有份量。我們每一件禮服都很獨特。比方說，這套 2 件式婚紗是目前最受歡迎的款式。及地的蕾絲長裙和短版上衣，非常適合新潮的新娘。

Possible answer 2

Ⓐ That's very kind of you. We have wedding dresses for everyone because we adore individuality. If you are a traditional bride, we have an elegantly fitted chiffon wedding dress with crystal embroidery at the waist. If you are having a destination wedding, this 1960 inspired vintage wedding gown is romantic with details and easy to transport.

真好。我們有適合每一種新娘的婚紗禮服，因為我們很重視個人特質。如果你喜歡傳統的婚禮，我們有一件優雅的雪紡婚紗，腰部還有優雅的水晶刺繡。如果你要辦海外婚禮，你

可以選擇這個設計靈感來自於 1960 年的復古婚紗，非常浪漫，也方便攜帶。

特助補給單字

clutch *n.* 手拿包

exotic *adj.* 異國情調的

embellishment *n.* 裝飾品

bucket *n.* 桶

crop *v.* 剪短的

 秘書特助對答技巧提點

The bucket bag was crafted from a supple textured leather with a wide wrist strap.

➲ Be crafted from... 以某物手工製作。例 1：This spoon was crafted from an old piece of furniture. （這個湯匙是由一塊舊家具製作而成的。）

This bag was used in NY fashion week as the after party gift bag, loaded with goodies such as a Chanel eye pencil, Dior red lipstick and our spring line of hand cream.

⊃ Be loaded with 裝滿了……。用來形容擺滿了，幾乎要裝不下的感覺。例 1：The pizza is loaded with seafood toppings and cheese.（比薩上擺滿了海鮮配料和乳酪。）例 2：My trunk was loaded with marketing materials, balloons and flowers.（我的後車箱裝滿了行銷輔銷物、氣球和鮮花。）

 ## 秘書特助經驗分享

　　如果你任職的精品品牌，展示空間超過一百坪以上的話，建議帶媒體參觀的時候，先分區講解。若是以品牌分區，可先簡單的介紹品牌核心精神，再挑一樣具代表性的產品，加強媒體對此品牌的印象。一次給太多訊息，對方反而會容易一頭霧水。也可以先觀察對方反應，如果有特別喜歡的物件，再給予詳盡的產品介紹也不遲喔！

年度媒體規劃與預算控制
Annual media planning and budget control

 秘書特助工作內容介紹

　　每一年的媒體預算該怎樣衡量好呢？以一個年度業績目標 2000 萬的公司來說，就至少要準備 200 萬的行銷預算。行銷費用最基本的額度就是年度業績的百分之十。如果行銷預算緊縮，很多通路行銷與公關媒體的操作將會受侷限，很有可能影響業績狀況。尤其是精品業與時尚產業，流行性質高，產品生命週期也短，如果品牌在媒體上曝光減少，很容易會被競爭對手的行銷活動給淹沒，漸漸被消費者淡忘。媒體預算不多的品牌，可以考慮發展多元通路與多元化的行銷方式。

職場上實況對談的一問二答 Track 36

每個行業的銷售旺季都不同，因此年度行銷活動的規劃方式，要依照新品研發與進入市場的時間來作規劃。讓我們透過以下 Amilia 與行銷部 Marketing 的問答，來更瞭解時尚業的年度行銷企劃吧！

Question 1

Ⓜ **Today we will finalize the marketing campaign chart and submit it for approval in order to get the marketing expenses. Are there any modifications that you would suggest before we send it to the Management Department?**

今天我們的年度行銷規劃表得做出定案，以提交審核行銷預算。在發送給管理部之前，你們有任何修改的建議嗎？

Possible answer 1

Ⓐ I have a suggestion; the marketing campaign has included magazine ads, channel marketing, customer services and charity sponsorship. I would like to suggest cutting down the magazine ads by 50% and redirecting the budget to the online marketing campaign.

我有一個想法，目前的行銷活動已經包括雜誌廣告、通路行銷、客戶服務和慈善機構的贊助。我想建議削減 50%的雜誌廣告，轉投資到網路行銷活動。

Possible answer 2

Ⓐ Yes, I do. I would like to propose adding funding to holding workshops or VIP parties in our brand stores. The goal is to attract potential customers to visit our stores. Our sales revenue has been compromised by the growing habit of online shopping. We need to remind our customers of the value of being in a store and the benefits of coming to the store instead of sitting at home making a transaction.

好的，我有個建議。我想建議增加預算在我們的品牌專賣店舉辦講座或 VIP 派對。目標是吸引潛在客戶參觀我們的商店。我們的銷售收入已經因為網路購物的盛行而受到影響。我們需要提醒消費者實體商店的價值，來店消費絕對比在家裡進行網路消費來的好。

Question 2

Ⓜ This year we have invested most of our marketing budget on branding, and social media. The result of our marketing research shows that our co-marketing campaign strengthens our brand recognition by 25%. The lifestyle concept is helping our image and sales revenue. Any ideas about large-scale events that we can step foot in?

今年我們投入了大部分的行銷預算在強化品牌和社群媒體上。而我們的市場調查結果顯示，異業結合讓我們品牌知名度上升了 25%。我覺得整體生活風格的形象對我們的業績很有幫助，這類型的大型活動你們有什麼點子嗎？

Possible answer 1

Ⓐ I suggest that in each season we outreach to a new audience. For example, in the spring, we could do co-marketing with Alisan flower viewing season, so our brand image will be associated with the beauty of nature and culture.

我建議每季和新群眾作接觸。例如，春季我們可以和阿里山賞花季作結合，讓品牌與自然和文化做連結。

Possible answer 2

Ⓐ I think it's time to start our own annual fashion festival! We can hold an event like a trunk show to reveal our fashion attire, as well as invite other successful brands in food, technology, wine or sport equipment industry. This will really help us develop the "lifestyle" concept.

我認為創造我們的時尚市集時候到了！我們可以每年舉辦活動，以搶先看的方式展示時尚穿搭，以及邀請其他行業內成功的品牌如食品、科技、葡萄酒或運動器材等。這可以幫助我們落實「生活風格」的概念。

秘書特助篇 ①

秘書特助行銷公關篇 ②

> 特助補給單字

transaction *n.* 買賣

outreach *v.* 拓展

 秘書特助對答技巧提點

Today we will finalize the marketing campaign chart and submit it for approval in order to get the marketing expenses.

➲ Finalize 最終確認；定稿。例 1：I can't leave on time today because I need to finalize the ad campaign.（我今天沒辦法準時下班，因為我要為廣告稿作最後的定稿。）例 2：The transaction is finally finalized after 2 hours of application.（這筆交易在 2 小時的冗長申請後，終於敲定了。）

Are there any modifications that you would suggest before we send to the Management Department?

➲ Modification 修改。例 1：Your public relation campaign requires some modifications. For example, the celebrity concert endorsement will definitely be eliminated.（你的公關活動需要做一些修改，例如名人演唱會的贊助絕對會被取消。）例 2：After mild modifications, the prototype was sent to the exhibit.（經過微調後，樣品就被送到展場了。）

秘書特助經驗分享

　　以時尚業來說，國際各大時尚週是採購的重要時間點之一，因此相關的行銷規劃會依照採購的新品進入銷售據點的時間來作配合。時尚業還要注重季節的問題，隨著換季，通常會有促銷活動來消化庫存，預留庫存空間待新商品入荷。消化舊貨庫存等於企業能夠獲得更多現金流，公司的整體運作也能更順利喔！

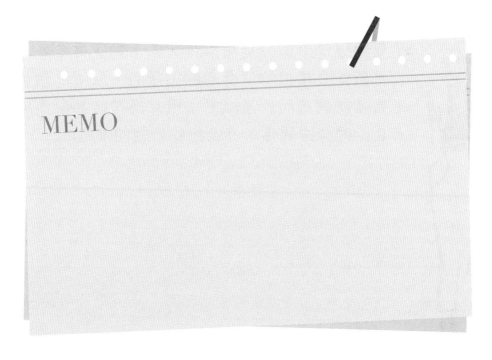

MEMO

UNIT 13 行銷輔銷物企劃與採購

Designing marketing materials and purchasing

 秘書特助工作內容介紹

　　行銷公關每天需要與媒體、廠商或重要客戶聯繫，在這些工作的背後，都是為了加強品牌對大眾的溝通與企業精神的傳達。每年的行銷輔銷物企劃，就是要增加品牌的能見度。比方說印有企業 LOGO 的購物袋、隨身碟，或是活動禮贈品。每年行銷部會絞盡腦汁製作行銷品，除了要幫助經銷商與分店增加銷售或活動宣傳之外，也得製作直接送給消費者的小禮品，以增加消費者對品牌的認同與忠誠度。因此與禮贈品廠商擁有良好的合作關係，亦是行銷公關的要務之一。

職場上實況對談的一問二答　◉ Track 37

除了禮贈品廠商，時尚業的行銷公關，也經常與印刷廠有密切接觸。例如製作公司的型錄，或是印刷企業對外使用的信封。另外還有場地的聯絡，與活動公司的交涉或是參展單位的溝通，都會是由公關一手包辦，如果你很喜歡與人溝通，那麼公關行銷這個工作會非常適合你。以下是 Amilia 與印刷廠業務 Sales 與禮品廠商 Alonso 之間的問答：

Question 1

🆂 **Hi, Amilia. I am calling to let you know that we are printing the branded corporate paper bag in 3 different volumes today. Would you like to come down to the factory to confirm the colors?**

嗨，愛蜜莉亞，我打電話來是要讓你知道，我們今天要印刷貴公司 3 個不同大小的企業紙袋。你想過來工廠確認印刷的顏色嗎？

Possible answer 1

🅐 Yes, our corporate color is a very distinct green with a hint of blue; I will bring a printout from our office as a sample. Also, can we discuss our next project while we are waiting for the printing machine to adjust the colors?

好的，我們的企業識別色是稍微帶藍調的特別綠色，我會從辦公室帶一份，我們自己列印顏色作為範本。另外，我們可

以在等待印刷機調整顏色的時候,順便討論我們下一個專案嗎?

Possible answer 2

Ⓐ Oh no, I have to be in a meeting all day. I am afraid I can't make it today. However, I will send our graphic designer over. She is responsible for our corporate image, so she is more than qualified to approve the color.

哦,糟糕,我今天恐怕沒辦法過去,我今天一整天都要開會。不過,我會派我們的平面設計師過去。她負責設計我們的企業形象,讓她確認顏色絕對綽綽有餘。

Question 2

Ⓜ Hi, Amilia. This is Alonso. How are you doing? We have a few new gifts and merchandise options available right now. Do you mind if I bring you a few samples and the new catalogue to you some time this week?

嗨!愛蜜莉亞,妳好嗎?我是阿隆索,我們公司現在新進了一些禮物和商品的選擇。你介意我這週找個時間,把新的樣品和型錄送過去給妳嗎?

Possible answer 1

Ⓐ Not at all. For the new marketing campaign, we are donating office stationery to public schools, so I could use a few new items to spice up the campaign. Also, do you have any new designs for the USB flash drives? We are running out of them and this time we want a USB flash drive in a shape of a key with our logo on it.

當然歡迎。今年全新的行銷活動，我們準備要捐贈辦公用品給公立學校，所以我想我會需要一些新品來豐富這次的活動內容。另外，你們有新款的隨身碟嗎？我們的隨身碟都快發完了，這一次我們希望作一款鑰匙形狀的隨身碟，上面印刷我們的商標。

Possible answer 2

Ⓐ Thank you so much, Alonso. However, I am totally swamped with the new marketing campaign and the upcoming event that we need to plan. Would you be so kind and send me the samples now?

非常感謝你，因為行銷專案的企劃和近期活動需要規劃，我完全沒有空閒的時間。可以先麻煩您寄樣品給我就好嗎？

▌特助補給單字

volume *n.* 容量

hint *n.* 微量

spice *v.* 使增添趣味

秘書特助對答技巧提點

She is responsible for our corporate image, so she is more than qualified to approve the color.

- Be qualified to ... 有資格去做……。

  例：Having been a publicist for more than 10 years, he is definitely qualified to take this job.

  （他當公關有十年以上的時間了，絕對有資格可以勝任這個工作。）

We are running out of them and this time we want a USB flash drive in a shape of a key with our logo on it.

- Be running out of 指即將用盡。例 1：I can't possibly purchase the front cover as we are running out of marketing fund.（我不可能買下雜誌封面，因為我們的行銷預算都快用完了。）例 2：We are running out of hotel options because we only got 2 weeks left before our departure.（我們已經沒有太多的飯店選擇，因為再兩週我們就要出發了。）

秘書特助經驗分享

　　公關經常替企業做採購，因此會結識許多廠商。過年、過節的時候，臺灣廠商通常都習慣會送禮。如果能夠婉拒是最好，以免以後在工作上多了人情壓力。如果對方十分堅持，最好是在大家在場的時候收下禮盒，並跟大家一起分享，以避免影響專業的形象，還有職場上的閒言閒語喔！

MEMO

秘書特助工作內容介紹

　　時尚公關負責所有對外的溝通，當然也包括社群網站與企業網站的文字內容（**A publicist has to maintain and write the content of the corporate website.**）。如果是代理國外品牌，也會是由公關與國外廠商聯繫，取得官方的圖片、產品介紹、型錄與樣品等資料，再由公關翻譯成合適的內容更新在公司網站上。對於網站資料定期地更新維護，讓品牌形象保持在最佳狀態，並讓消費者維持對品牌的新鮮感，也是行銷公關的職責之一。品牌形象可以一季更新一次，而品牌的新聞稿與媒體曝光則是每個月都要補上最新動態。

職場上實況對談的一問二答

 Track 38

網站上的品牌內容還有企業故事、品牌精神、產品圖片、展示空間地址與照片，企業消息稿與新品新聞稿，這些內容也都是公關要獨立完成，因此公關時常要跨部門索取資料，或聘請攝影師做形象的拍攝。公關必須要具有美感與文字的靈敏度，才能把品牌經營的有聲有色。以下是 Amilia 與網站設計公司 Jacob 之間的問答。

Question 1

🇯 **Hi, Amilia. This is Jacob from Multimedia, Taiwan. Our annual service fee is due next week, so I would like to know if you would like to upgrade the corporate website before we send you the invoice.**

愛蜜莉亞您好，我是台灣多媒體的雅各。今年的服務費會在下週到期，所以我想在給您明年度帳單之前，詢問您是否需要企業網站升級。

Possible answer 1

🅰 Hi, Jacob. Thanks for the reminder. We are planning to renew the website technology since our current website isn't compatible with most mobile devices.

雅各，你好，感謝你的提醒。我們有計劃要更新網站的技術，因為我們目前的網站不支援大部份的行動裝置。

Possible answer 2

A Hi, Jacob. I was just about to call you because I have new product materials and media exposure for you to update today. There is no alteration needed, so you can go ahead and send us the invoice.

雅各，你好，我正要給你打電話呢！因為今天我有新的產品資料和媒體曝光要更新在網站上。目前的網站並不需要作改變，所以你可以直接把帳單寄過來了。

Question 2

J Hi, Amilia. Did you want to talk to me about adding a feature on your website? We can deliver a tailored solution for any requests that you may have.

嗨！愛蜜莉亞，您想和我談您的網站上增加一個功能？我們可以為您的任何要求提供量身訂制的解決方案。

Possible answer 1

A I need customized software that analyzes consumer behavior online. We want to know who browses our website, which content is the most popular, and when they visit it.

我需要訂製線上分析消費者行為的軟體。我們想知道誰瀏覽我們的網站，哪些內容是最受歡迎的，以及瀏覽者會在什麼時段拜訪我們的網站。

Possible answer 2

🅐 Our online shopping has grown so much over the years. Now, we want to manage product lead time, delivery date, and stock levels at the same time. We need to cut down the manual procedures to speed up the purchase orders. Could you program easygoing online software that improves the quality of our online shopping experience?

我們的網上購物增長如此之快，多年來，現在我們要在同一時間來管理產品交貨時間、交貨日期和庫存水平。我們需要削減人工手續，加快採購訂單。你能設計容易操作，且改善線上購物經驗的軟體嗎？

特助補給單字

alteration *n.* 更改

tailored *adj.* 訂做的

秘書特助對答技巧提點

Our annual service fee is due next week, so I would like to know if you would like to upgrade the corporate website before we send you the invoice.

- ⊃ Be due 到期、應支付的、預定的。例 1：My phone bill is due in 2 days.（我的手機帳單再過兩天就要過期了。）例 2：Her baby is due in 2 months.（她的小孩再過兩個月就要生了。）

- ⊃ Invoice and receipt 發票與收據。這兩個單字經常會被搞混，當你是廠商要開發票過去請款的時候，你是要開 invoice，而你消費完要拿的收據是 receipt，不要記錯囉！例：I forgot to ask the accountant to issue an invoice to claim the payment.（我忘了請會計幫我開發票，好讓我要求付款。）

We need to cut down the manual procedures to speed up the purchase orders.

- ⊃ Cut down 削減或縮短。例 1：We need to cut down expenses and create more income.（我們需要削減開支，創造更多的收入。）例 2： I need to cut down my intake of sugar in order to lose weight.（我需要減少我的糖分攝取，以減輕我的體重。）

秘書特助經驗分享

　　網站定期做維護更新可以讓潛在客戶不需要到店裡就瞭解品牌的風格主軸。目前許多時尚網站增加了互動軟體，目的是延長顧客停留在網站的時間；或是增加即時線上通訊軟體，讓客戶可以馬上針對產品問題得到解答。有的購物網站增加了時尚秀的功能，以動態的方式展現服裝配件，針對高級服飾在網路購買卻無法試穿的問題，為客戶提供貼心的協助。

❶ 秘書特助篇

❷ 秘書特助行銷公關篇

MEMO

UNIT 15 社群網站更新與維護
Updating and maintaining social networks

秘書特助工作內容介紹

　　這幾年來社群網站的發達，使得公關也進入這個領域，多了一個品牌行銷的工具。越是活用不同的行銷方式，越能維持消費者對品牌的新鮮感（Juggle between multiple marketing tools such as innovative social media management is a key for successful branding.）現在大家都使用社群網站，是這個產業無法忽視的事實。社群網站的立即性有其他媒體無法取代的優勢。倚賴視覺的時尚產業，受到社群網站的幫助，讓品牌視覺與產品的穿搭，隨著使用者的轉發而快速蔓延。因此經營品牌社群網站，的確是能夠有效培養忠實客戶的方法之一。

職場上實況對談的一問二答

 Track 39

時尚公關可以透過社群網站，以圖片的方式透露品牌的內幕。重點是要上傳一眼就吸引人的內容。社群網站不適合複雜的資料，公關也能比較輕鬆地操作這個平台。目前的社群網站種類眾多，也衍生出社群網站公關（social media publicist）這個專業。以下是 Amilia 與面試者 Mose 的問答：

Question 1

Ⓜ Thank you for giving me an opportunity to meet with you. I have heard a lot about you, and I hope I can assist you with branding and much more. Should I start with a self-introduction?

謝謝你給我一個見面的機會。我久仰大名，我很希望可以幫助你和品牌的推廣。我應該先自我介紹嗎？

Possible answer 1

Ⓐ No, that won't be necessary. I have a pretty good idea about your past experience. I am impressed with your work in social media. Since I have a pretty full plate myself, I need someone to manage our social media for the brand.

不，暫時不需要，我很清楚你的履歷。我對於你在社交媒體方面的經驗有深刻的印象。因為我的工作滿檔，我需要有人來管理我們品牌的社群媒體。

Possible answer 2

🄰 We can do that a little later. Your background in social media management is what got you the interview today. If you are hired, what would be your first approach to social media? I feel like social media will allow us to be accessible, so you will also be responsible for customer service that comes from social media.

這之後再做也不遲。你管理社交媒體的經驗讓你得到今天的面試。我希望你能告訴我們，如果你被錄用，你在社交媒體經營上會做的第一件事是什麼。社群網站讓我們與消費者的距離更近，所以你也將負責來自這些平台的客戶服務。

Question 2

🄼 **I would suggest first establishing official Facebook and Instagram accounts. Facebook comes with site analysis that you can monitor and ad purchase is also available. With our colorful clothing line and the creative campaign, being on Instagram will attract a lot of followers. Are you also an active user of both social media sites?**

我會建議首先建立一個官方的臉書和 Instagram 帳號。臉書有社群分析，你可以監控帳號的活動，也可以購買廣告。我們品牌豐富多彩又有創意的服裝，在 Instagram 上可以吸引很多追隨者。您也是社交媒體活躍的使用者嗎？

Possible answer 1

🅐 Yes, I am. I think Facebook can provide more information about our brand, which has another demographic of followers.

對，我是 Instagram 的重度用戶。我認為臉書能夠提供更多品牌資訊，那邊的粉絲群眾會是另外一個族群。

Possible answer 2

🅐 Yes, I am but I rarely have time to upload anything myself. I browse them on my phone during my morning commute. I think getting to know our target audience will give you a better idea about which social media would be the best for our brand. Pace yourself. Start with no more than 2 social media and develop from there.

是的，但我很少有時間上傳。早晨的通勤時間我會用手機瀏覽。我想，充分了解我們的目標群眾，會幫助我們找出最適合我們品牌的社交媒體。你不用操之過急，一開始不要超過 2 個社群網站，再從那裡慢慢發展。

▌特助補給單字

plate *n.* 盤子

monitor *v.* 監控

pace *v.* 慢慢地走

秘書特助對答技巧提點

I have a pretty good idea about your past experience.

⊃ have an idea about something 瞭解某件事情。例：I might <u>have an idea about</u> how to cook this dish.（我可能對如何煮這道菜略知一二。）

Since I have a pretty full plate myself, I need someone to manage our social media for the brand.

⊃ a full plate 字面上的意思是「裝滿食物的盤子」，但這片語代表的，是很忙碌的意思，幾乎忙不過來的狀態。例：I know you <u>have a full plate</u> right now, but I am still hoping you can make it to family reunion dinner.（我知道你最近真的很忙，但我還是希望你可以來參加家族聚餐。）

秘書特助經驗分享

　　社群網站中常見的除了常用的 Facebook、Instagram，還有 Twitter、Pinterest……等。共通點除了都方便在手機等智慧型裝置上操作之外，在運用的性質上是有些許的不同的。臉書是目前時尚產業最普遍使用的平台，現在各大品牌也都慢慢開始使用 IG。會使用這些社群網站對公關來說是基本的功課，所以你今天# hashtag 了嗎？

❶ 秘書特助篇

❷ 秘書特助行銷公關篇

MEMO

UNIT 16 活動派對統籌與團隊調配

Coordinating events and manpower

秘書特助工作內容介紹

　　時尚公關經常辦活動，從活動的發想到執行，擔任活動統籌中最重要的角色（A publicist in the fashion industry is often the event planner who puts together an event from concept through completion.）。如果你喜歡熱鬧又注重細節，你會很適合擔任公關。熱鬧的活動背後，是冗長的事前準備，包括邀請函的印刷與設計、燈光與音樂的準備、會場租借與佈置。如果有異業結合，你要負責聯繫商品的運送與退還。在活動當天的人手安排、確認所有流程都順暢，活動接近尾聲時，你也許有空稍微享受這一切。公關就是這樣忙碌的工作，但成就感也成正比。

職場上實況對談的一問二答　 Track 40

❶ 秘書特助篇

❷ 秘書特助行銷公關篇

除了會場的準備之外，公關還有招待貴賓還有長官的重責大任。無論對內對外，公關都需要良好的 EQ 與超強的組織能力，讓公司同仁的階段性任務更順利。與大家和樂相處，活動啟動的時候，大家也會更願意全力協助你喔！以下是 Amilia 與公司同事 John 的問答：

Question 1

🄒 **Amilia, the Sales Department is really counting on you for their 15ᵗʰ anniversary party; all of our dealers will fly to Taipei and join this event. How can we cooperate with you in order to make this event a success?**

愛蜜莉亞，我們所有的經銷商都會飛來台北參加 15 週年晚會，這個活動業務部門就指望妳了。為了讓這個活動成功，我們可以怎樣協助妳？

Possible answer 1

🄐 That's the spirit, John! First of all, I would like to confirm the number of guests each of you may invite. I haven't gotten all the feedback since we send out the party invitations. I will need things by the end of the week to secure catering and seating arrangements.

約翰，你這樣的態度就對了！首先我想確認你們每個人要邀請的客戶人數；派對邀請函送出去之後，我還沒收到所有的回函。最晚這週前得確認餐飲和座位的安排。

Possible answer 2

🅐 That means a lot to me, thanks. At the reception, I will need all of you to make sure the guests drop their business cards into the lucky draw box. I am sure you don't want your valuable customers to miss the chance to win the grand prize.

你能這樣想真好，謝謝。於接待處，我需要你們確保所有來賓都把名片放入抽獎箱。我相信你不會想讓重要的客戶錯過贏得大獎的機會。

Question 2

🅙 **Hi, Amilia. I have sent you the list of our guests and the total is 100 people. Could you send the hotel accommodation e-mail to me again? I might have deleted it by accident.**

嗨，愛蜜莉亞，我已經把客人名單寄給妳了，客人總計為 **100** 位。你能再把飯店住宿安排的電子郵件發給我嗎？我好像不小心誤刪了。

Possible answer 1

🅐 Thanks a lot, and I will have my secretary send you the e-mail again. Since we are on this subject, I am considering renting a bus to take our guests from the hotel to the party location. However, I am not sure if your sales teams have other arrangements.

非常謝謝你，我會請助理再把信發給您。既然我們在這個話題上，我正在考慮是否要租巴士，把客人飯店送到派對的場地。但我不知道你的業務團隊是否有其他安排？

Possible answer 2

🄰 Thank you, John. I really appreciate your efficiency. During the party, we will have a hand in the "wax hand" activity that our dealers and customers can enjoy. The wax hand party favor with their 15th anniversary corporate logo needs a day to air out and dry completely. Therefore, if your guests are leaving the next day, please make sure you have their correct addresses, so we can mail them their souvenirs from the party.

謝謝你約翰，你真的很有效率。在晚會上，我們的經銷商和客戶都可以參加製作蠟手模型的活動。印有公司成立 15 週年標誌的模型需要一整天才能風乾。如果你的客人第二天要馬上離開，請記下對方的正確地址，以利我們郵寄紀念品給他們。

特助補給單字

anniversary *n.* 紀念日

spirit *n.* 精神

catering *n.* 外燴

souvenir *n.* 紀念品

 秘書特助對答技巧提點

The Sales Department is really counting on you for their 15th anniversary party.

➲ Count on someone 完全信賴／依靠某人。例 1：I am counting on you to perform for 100 people tomorrow night!（明天晚上就靠你表演給 100 個人看了！）例 2：Taking into consideration that she has always been late, I guess I can't count on her to bring us the train tickets.（考慮到她一向愛遲到，我想我不能指望她帶火車票給我們。）

That's the spirit, John!

➲ 這句話常被用來鼓勵好的行為，或好的態度。That's the spirit! After 10 phone calls, the brand manager still doesn't answer her call, but she is not even close to giving up.（就是這種屹立不搖的精神！經過 10 通電話，品牌經理還是不願意接她電話，但她完全沒有要放棄的意思。）

秘書特助經驗分享

　　公關是個需要跨部門協調的職位，每個部門都會有自己堅持的立場，在這之中取得平衡點，舉辦大家皆大歡喜的活動，不是一件容易的事情。身為公關必須抗壓力強，協調能力好，當衝突無法解決的時候，只要把持住公司的最大利益，就以你覺得最好的方式去處理吧！一個統籌者必須要堅定立場，其他人才知道該如何配合你。

MEMO

協助行銷活動與執行
Assisting marketing activities and implementation

 ## 秘書特助工作內容介紹

　　公關與行銷部通常是被編列在同一個部門，因為台灣的企業通常把企業形象與產品行銷混合操作，然而公關與行銷的內容其實細分下來，是兩種不同的專業。公關是企業對外的形象與窗口，所以公關的工作內容是溝通與呈現品牌。而行銷企劃則是負責新品上市活動、通路經營、產品包裝與定價策略等面向的工作內容。以公司的大型活動來說，如果是以提升品牌為主，就會是以公關為統籌，其他部門提供協助。反之，若是以業務或行銷部主辦的活動，公關也會出席效力。

職場上實況對談的一問二答　 Track 41

以業務部舉辦的經銷商大會，或是以行銷部舉辦與產品相關的活動，公關通常可以協助招待國外廠商與會場佈置，以公關擅長的工作項目，跨部門提供活動支援。以下是公關 Amilia 與行銷部 Marketing Department 的問答內容：

Question 1

M **Hi, Amilia. Thank you for coming to our marketing meeting. As you know our signature engagement ring collection is going to hold a private party in our flagship store. We can use your suggestions for setting up the event, such as catering and florist recommendations.**

嗨，愛蜜莉亞，感謝您來參加我們的行銷會議。正如你所知道的，我們準備要在旗艦店舉行我們經典款訂婚戒指的私人鑑賞派對。在會場佈置的部分，例如餐飲、花店，我們在想或許能採用您的建議。

Possible answer 1

A You are very welcome. Thank you for inviting me. I have a fantastic catering company that you can get in touch with. In fact, I can ask them to design a drink menu that is named after our collection, as well as finger food suitable for an engagement party. You want to make them feel special in this party.

不用客氣，謝謝您邀請我。我推薦一間很棒的餐飲公司，你可以跟他們聯繫。事實上，我想要求他們設計一個以我們戒款命名的飲品，以及能在訂婚派對上看到的餐點，好讓客戶覺得倍受寵愛。

Possible answer 2

Ⓐ I am happy to be here because I enjoy planning parties. I like the idea of holding an exclusive event for our most valuable customers. I believe it will have a positive influence on our brand image. May I suggest having the florist make a small bouquet as a party gift. This will definitely encourage them to post photos on social media.

我很高興來到這裡，因為我喜歡策劃派對。為重要客戶舉辦獨家活動的這個想法我覺得很棒。我相信這將會對我們的品牌形象產生正面的影響。我建議請花店做一個小花束送給每個來賓，這必定會鼓勵他們上傳照片到社交媒體網站。

Question 2

Ⓜ Hi, Amilia. We are helping the Sales Department to put together a dealer conference. We are a bit understaffed at the moment. Do you think you can help us out on that day?

嗨！愛蜜莉亞，我們正在幫助業務部舉辦經銷商大會。目前我們人手不足，請問您那天可以支援我們嗎？

Possible answer 1

🅐 Of course. Just let me know when and where. I can help you design the invitation card if you want. Please provide the goal of the event, the target audience, time and location.

當然，請讓我知道時間和地點就好。如果你有需要，我還可以幫你設計邀請卡，只要你提供受邀者的基本資料、時間、地點、活動主旨，還有會議預計進行的時間。

Possible answer 2

🅐 I can do better than that. I have been to a couple of dealer conferences. I think I can help you set up the product display station. We have made a few custom-made acrylic display stands from our previous events. I can lay out a few designs for you and see if they are useful for you.

我可以提供更多的協助喔！我曾經參加過幾次經銷商會議，我可以幫你設置產品展示架。以前辦活動的時候，我們有一些訂製的壓克力陳列架。我可以列出一些選項給你，看看是否適用。

> **特助補給單字**

engagement *n.* 訂婚

bouquet *n.* 花束

acrylic *adj.* 壓克力的

lay *v.* 放置

 秘書特助對答技巧提點

I have a fantastic catering company that you can get in touch with.

⊃ Get in touch with someone 與某人取得聯繫。例：Could you get in touch with our landlord and discuss the condition of the apartment with him, please?（可以麻煩您盡快與我們的房東聯絡，並與他討論公寓目前的情況嗎？）

⊃ 相似的片語尚有 Keep in touch or stay in touch 保持聯繫。例：Please keep in touch with me while you are travelling around the world.（在你旅行世界各地的時候，請和我保持聯絡。）

I can ask them to design a drink menu that is named after our collection, as well as finger food suitable for an engagement party.

⊃ Be named after 以……命名。Name something 為……命名。例 1：I purchased a star and named it after you.（我購買了天上的一顆星星，以你為名。）例 2：My son is named after my father, while his middle name is named after my great grandfather.（我的兒子以我父親的名字命名，而他的中間的小名則是以我的曾祖父命名。）

 ## 秘書特助經驗分享

　　公關因為經常舉辦活動以及採購企業禮贈品與行銷輔銷物的工作，會認識許多優質廠商。在其他部門辦活動的時候，通常都可以為大家提出一些不錯的點子，或是協助處理外包廠商之間的聯絡。因為擅長與人溝通，亦可幫忙擔任主持人，讓活動流程更順暢。公關在公司裡的角色，總是擁有彈性與豐富的工作性質。

產品外拍與品牌精神掌握

Arranging commercial photography that captures the brand identity

 ## 秘書特助工作內容介紹

　　公關除了主動提供品牌資訊與高解析的圖片給媒體之外，有時候也會收到媒體產品借出或是外借場地的邀約。公關要確保產品借出不會受到損壞、報導主題符合品牌精神，以及拍攝的的品質把關與拍攝期間所有的聯絡與運送，都是由公關一手包辦。雜誌編輯與記者經常需要人物專訪與產品拍攝的場地，如果你願意出借你美輪美奐的展示空間，公關通常也會從中協助，以換取店家與品牌在媒體上的曝光機會。媒體需要公關在拍攝過程中引導品牌的呈現方式，以最大化媒體報導的力量。

職場上實況對談的一問二答　　⊙ Track 42

媒體的文字敘述需要公關給予正確的品牌與產品介紹，而產品拍攝的部分則要視公關的美感與對品牌精神的掌握度，最後的報導才能感動人心。以下是 Amilia 與雜誌社 Twyla 的對話問答。

Question 1

🅣 **Hi, Amilia. This is Twyla from Urban magazine. I have a proposition for you. We are going to interview successful female entrepreneurs, and we need a modern interior that fits their image and accentuates their feminism. So I thought of your beautiful showroom. Do you think we can arrange for our interviews and photo sessions to be held in your showroom?**

嗨！愛蜜莉亞，我是城市雜誌的萃拉。我有一個提議，我們想要面試成功的女強人，我們想強調他們的女權主義所以認為現代化的空間最符合她們的形象。因此我認為你們美麗的展示空間很適合這個主題，你覺得我們可以在那邊安排採訪和攝影嗎？

Possible answer 1

🅐 Hey, Twyla. I am definitely interested. However, we have a new product launch event and a pop-up store event in the next 2 weeks, so our showroom won't be available until the end of the month. Also, we usually have a rental fee because the photo session might affect our customers. I can waive the rental fee for you if you can guarantee media exposure that values up to 2 thousand dollars.

嗨，萃拉，我很有興趣。但未來 2 個星期內，我們有新品推出還有快閃店的活動，所以我們的店內空間直到月底前都無法借出。此外，我們通常有場地租賃費，因為拍照可能會影響我們的來店客戶。如果你可以提供價值 2 千美元以上的媒體曝光，我可以幫您免除這項費用。

Possible answer 2

🄰 Hello, Twyla. I am flattered that you have thought of us for the photo shoot. This article certainly speaks to our target audience. We will be delighted to help out. Actually, as long as our brand and the store location will be mentioned in the article, we are more than happy to offer the clothing sponsorship for the photo shoot.

您好、萃拉，我很榮幸您想到了我們。這篇文章的內容正中我們的目標客群，我們很高興可以提供您協助。事實上，只要我們的品牌和店家住址在文章中能被提及，我們願意為這次的拍攝提供服裝贊助。

Question 2

🅣 Hi, Amilia. I've got your newsletter about the new fragrance and thank you so much for the sample. The aroma reminds me of a breezy spring morning. In the next issue, we are recommending luxury fragrances and skin care products for debutantes to balls in Asia. Could you send over your list of recommended products for the photo shoot?

嗨！愛蜜莉亞，我收到了你寄來的香水新品新聞稿還有樣品。香氣讓我想到吹著微風的春天早晨。下一期我們打算推薦適合亞洲社交名媛舞會的名貴香水和保養品。可以請您推薦一些產品過來，讓我們拍攝嗎？

Possible answer 1

A: Hi, Twyla. I love your expression when you wear the new fragrance! I am thinking of the "ELLE" collection will be a good choice for debutantes. A refined perfume bottle holding the scent of water lilies, green tea and rose, the soft; those refreshing perfumes represent young minds and spirits.

嗨，萃拉，我喜歡你噴上新款香水的表情！我想到「ELLE系列」將是社交名媛們一個不錯的選擇。精緻的香水瓶帶著睡蓮、綠茶和玫瑰的香氣；那些清新的香水代表著幼小的心靈和精神。

Possible answer 2

Ⓐ You are very welcome. I am glad you enjoy the fragrance. We have a new skin care product made from herbal extracts and shimmering pearls. The premium facial treatment will revitalize and hydrate any skin type, which is perfect for a debutante who wants to look radiant on the big day.

非常歡迎，很高興你喜歡那個香味。我們有一項新的皮膚護理產品，由天然草本植物萃取物和珍珠提煉而成。頂級臉部護理將活化和滋潤任何皮膚類型，非常適合想在重大日子看起來容光煥發的名媛使用。

特助補給單字

proposition *n.* 提議

accentuate *v.* 強調

feminism *n.* 女性主義

waive *v.* 減免

 秘書特助對答技巧提點

I can waive the rental fee for you if you can guarantee media exposure that value up to 2 thousand dollars.

⊃ Waive 撤回、不強求執行。例 1：I waived my complaint to the hotel because they fully compensate my hotel fee and transportation to the airport.（我放棄投訴這家酒店，因為他們完全賠償我的住宿旅費用和來回機場的交通費用。）例 2：Could you <u>waive</u> my student meal plan because I am living off campus this year.（請撤回我的學生膳食費用，因為我今年不住學校宿舍。）

The premium facial treatment will revitalize and hydrates any skin type, which is perfect for a debutante who wants to look radiant on the big day.

- Premium 最高價，最優質的。例：Please enjoy the fruit wine made from <u>premium</u> peaches and plums.（請享受我們用最頂級的蜜桃和李子做成的水果酒。）
- Revitalize 活化。例：This detox water will <u>revitalize</u> your body and your skin will glow the next morning.（這排毒水可以活化你的身體，第二天早上你的皮膚會顯亮。）

 秘書特助經驗分享

　　當然在外借商品與場地外借的部分，公關不見得需要照單全收。比方說產品過於貴重或脆弱不適合出借，或是與形象不符合的主題與刊物，都有可能在衡量之後婉拒對方。如果主題符合，公關可以改以提供官方圖片或去背圖，透過後製的方式參與。為了顧全品牌形象，公關有職責要來保護公司產品與企業的最大利益。

危機處理

Crisis management

 秘書特助工作內容介紹

　　作為一個公關，你得懂得危機處理（Being a publicist, you must be ready to put out fires.）。公關總是積極對外宣傳品牌的優點，但越是壯大的企業，總有受到社會輿論壓力的時候。此時企業的處理方式，會受到大眾的放大檢視，可以左右一個企業的形象與日後的發展。因此平日就要有危機意識，把負面新聞的殺傷力降到最低。比方說客戶投訴或產品瑕疵，這些議題都很容易受到媒體注目。公關必須要第一時間妥善處理，如果企業願意承責任並且有誠意處理，很可以把劣勢反轉為優勢。

職場上實況對談的一問二答　 Track 43

如果負面新聞在社群網站上散播，公關必須在最短時間內作出回覆。回答的內容必須誠信，如果公司有錯，一定要先道歉，以安撫客戶的情緒。切記不能回覆「不予置評」，會讓企業顯得漠不關心客戶的權益。以下是公關 Amilia 與客戶 Customer 和媒體 Media 之間的問答：

Question 1

C I bought this pair of pants last week, and after I wore them, my skin had a serious allergic reaction to them. The discomfort continues, so I had to go to the doctor. I am horrified by the experience and I want to return this pair of pants right now.

我上週買了這條褲子，穿上後，我的皮膚嚴重過敏，一直很不舒服，所以我不得不去看醫生。我嚇壞了，我想馬上退回這條褲子。

Possible answer 1

A Absolutely. We sincerely apologize for this unfortunate incident. We will get to the bottom of this and that is a promise. I will not only refund you the full amount, but also would like to compensate you for your medical bills.

當然，我們真誠地為這一不幸事件深表歉意，我們會好好了解此事，這是一個承諾。我不僅將退還您全款，也將要提供支付您的醫療費用。

Possible answer 2

🅐 Hello, Ma'am. This is Amilia, the publicist of the brand. First of all, we are very sorry for this experience you had to go through. We understand it must have been very difficult. We have made an appointment for you at the nation's best dermatoglogy clinic. If you would like to go right now, we have everything arranged. If you prefer your own doctor, we are willing to accompany you and assist you in every way. Without a doubt, your money will be fully refunded to your credit card.

您好女士，我的名字是愛蜜莉亞，品牌的公關。首先，為您所經歷的這些，我們感到非常抱歉。我們知道那肯定是非常難受的。我們已經為您預約了全國最好的皮膚科診所。如果您想馬上去就醫，我們也安排好了一切。如果你喜歡自己的醫生，我們願意在各個方面提供您協助。毫無疑問，您的錢將全額退還到您的信用卡裡。

Question 2

🅝 Hey, Amilia. I have heard the news about someone who had an allergic reaction to one of

your products. You wouldn't mind if we conduct an interview at the shop, would you?

嗨！愛蜜莉亞，我聽到有人對您的產品有過敏反應的消息。你不會介意我們到店裡採訪吧？

Possible answer 1

Ⓐ Of course not. In fact, I am at the retail store right now. We have everything under control. The doctor has informed us that the condition is rather rare, but we have advised our production line to change the color formula to prevent the situation from happening again.

當然不會，其實我現在就在零售商店裡。一切都在我們的掌握中。醫生已通知我們，這樣的情況是相當罕見的，但我們已建議我們的生產線改變顏色配方，以防止這種情況的發生。

Possible answer 2

Ⓐ Thank you for asking and we are definitely up for an interview. The customer was very understanding and thoughtful. We are glad to inform you that her condition has improved and she no longer needs medication.

謝謝你的要求，我們非常願意接受採訪。客戶非常理解和體貼。我們很高興地通知你，她的病情有所好轉，不再需要接受治療。

特助補給單字

bottom *n.* 底部

medical *adj.* 醫學的

refund *v.* 退款

allergic *adj.* 過敏的

rare *adj.* 罕見的

 秘書特助對答技巧提點

We will get to the bottom of this and that is a promise.

‣ Get to the bottom of something 意指把一件事情查得水落石出，完全負責到底，不查清楚絕不罷休的意思。例：The teacher was determined to get to the bottom of who stole the exam papers. （老師下定決心要查清楚是誰偷走了考試卷。）

I have heard the news about someone who had an allergic reaction to one of your products.

‣ To have an allergic reaction to something 是指對某個物質或食物產生過敏反應。過敏反應也可以用 be allergic to something 這個用法；allergic reaction 指過敏反應。例：Itching, redness and irritation on the skin are very common allergic reactions. （皮膚瘙癢、紅腫和疼痛不適是很常見的過敏反應。）

秘書特助經驗分享

　　負面新聞出現時，官方聲明稿需要在最短時間內發出來，讓社會大眾覺得業者是重視消費者權益的。除了馬上止血，還可以請求平衡報導。還要請媒體報導關於企業的正面新聞（positive PR），以壓抑負面報導對於企業的不良影響。社會的輿論通常都有正反兩方，多去製造正面的新聞，對企業形象的損害就能減少。

MEMO

UNIT 20 藉由藝人和時尚模特兒宣傳品牌精神

Promoting brand image through performing artists and fashion models

 ## 秘書特助工作內容介紹

時尚單品如果透過名模或是明星的穿搭介紹，在他們的粉絲群眾中，品牌知名度就會瞬間提升。如果打對目標族群，粉絲們會互相討論、問問題，並在網路上轉貼，引起口碑行銷的效果。名人的知名度高，去哪都可能會有媒體跟拍，如果穿戴品牌的衣服飾品，很容易一併被報導。這與媒體的廣告採買不同，有著藝人的推薦加持與搭配示範，會比廣告更生活化。消費者會有效仿的心態，會想要找出這個產品的品牌和售價，如果有消費能力就很可能購買。

職場上實況對談的一問二答

Track 44

時尚公關也需要與藝人經紀、藝人與模特兒維持友好的關係，一來有機會為品牌在實體通路合作，為行銷廣告的拍攝鋪路，二來在社群網站的產品推薦上，品牌也能有曝光的機會。以下是 Amilia 與藝人明星 Celebrity 和模特兒 Model 之間的問答：

Question 1

C **Hi, Amilia. You never seem to miss any fashion events! No wonder I see your products everywhere. I love the red lipstick on your campaign ad. I would love to sample your cosmetics and share them with my Instagarm followers, what do you say?**

嗨，愛蜜莉亞，你似乎從來沒有錯過任何時尚活動！難怪我看到你的產品無處不在。我好喜歡妳們廣告上的那個紅色唇膏，我想在 Instagram 上面試用妳們的化妝品給我的粉絲們看和分享，你覺得呢？

Possible answer 1

A Say no more. I will send the red lipstick to you first thing in the morning. As for the rest of the beauty products, let me know your skin type, so I can send the skin care that's right for you. I can also prepare a set for your agent. Can I get your phone number or add your Line account? I think it's probably easier

271

to keep in touch that way.

我已經被你說服了，紅色唇膏明天一早上就會送去給你。保養品的話，請告訴我你的皮膚狀況，我才能把適合你的護膚產品送給你。我還可以準備一套給你的經紀人。我可以留你的電話號碼或加入你的 LINE 通訊帳號嗎？這樣聯絡起來更方便。

Possible answer 2

Ⓐ Who doesn't love parties? As for the product sampling, we are launching a new line of lip gloss that's very moisturizing to your lips and dries into a smooth, velvety texture that you have not seen before. How about I send you a full set of the new lip glosses?

誰不喜歡參加派對呢？試用產品的部分，我們剛推出了滋潤型的唇彩系列，擦上去後會轉化成前所未見的滑順天鵝絨質地。我先送你一整套的全新唇彩怎麼樣？

Question 2

Ⓜ Hi, Amilia. Thank you for the skin care products on my birthday. It was very thoughtful of you. I really like the soft jasmine smell and how it soothes my skin on a hot summer day. Are we expecting any new products this season?

嗨！愛蜜莉亞，謝謝妳特地送我生日禮物，妳真的很貼心。

我很喜歡那護膚產品淡淡的茉莉花香，在炎熱的夏天它能舒緩我的肌膚。妳們這一季還會有新產品嗎？

Possible answer 1

🅐 I am glad you like them. Yes, we have a sunscreen product in water base. It's clear and skin calming, leaving your face baby soft and refreshing.

我很高興你喜歡妳的禮物。有的，有一款水基底防曬產品，它透明純淨、鎮靜肌膚，讓妳的臉像嬰兒般柔軟。

Possible answer 2

🅐 You are very welcome; you are a dear friend of ours. Yes, we are launching an ingenious sunscreen lotion that protects your skin without the heavy feeling one usually gets from sunscreen. It's translucent and keeps your make-up in place. What more can you ask for on a hot summer day? I will send a sampler box for you ladies!

不用客氣，妳是我們的好朋友。是的，我們正要推出一個別出心裁的防曬霜，它保護妳的皮膚，卻不會像一般防曬乳給妳沉悶的感覺。它是半透明的，還可以讓妳不脫妝。在炎熱夏季所需要的不就是這個嗎？我會送一盒樣品過去給妳們的！

特助補給單字

sample *v.* 試用

moisturizing *adj.* 滋潤的

soothe *v.* 舒緩

ingenious *adj.* 製作精巧的

translucent *adj.* 半透明的

 秘書特助對答技巧提點

We are launching an ingenious sunscreen lotion that protects your skin without the heavy feeling one usually gets from sunscreen.

➲ Without 是介系詞，代表沒有的意思。接在後面的動詞記得要用 Ving。常見用法還有 do without 是「沒有……也可以」的意思。例 1：Our flight is boarding right now. If she doesn't come back in 5 minutes, we are leaving without her.（現在我們的航班在登機，如果 5 分鐘內她再不回來，我們就不等她了。）例 2：Chile is known for its sunny and dry weather; you can't go there without sunscreen.（智利的天氣是著名的晴朗乾燥，你絕對不能忘了防曬霜。）

It's translucent and keeps your make-up in place. What more can you ask for on a hot summer day?

● In place 恰當、在正確的地方。例 1：Everything is in place for the engagement party.（訂婚派對的準備一切就緒。）例 2：Your words of wisdom are in place.（你充滿智慧的發言真的很到位。）

 秘書特助經驗分享

　　贈送明星與藝人試用產品的時候，並不代表一定會被採用。越是有知名度的藝人，每天都會收到許多贈品，一定會優先發表付費的廠商。如果你正在宣傳知名度尚未打開的新品牌，你可以多花點心思讓送過去的包裹看起來更誘人。產品包裝設計也很重要，藝人粉絲雖用不到商品，卻看得到包裝視覺設計。只要你的產品能讓他們想多看兩眼，你就成功囉！

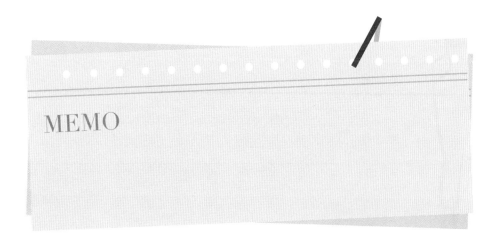

MEMO

UNIT 21 與部落客與造型師建立良好關係

Establishing good relationships with bloggers and stylists

秘書特助工作內容介紹

　　部落客文化隨著網路的發展，像雨後春筍般的出現。部落客扮演著業餘達人的角色，對自己鍾愛的主題在網路上進行圖片與文章的分享。很多時尚部落客，因為時常分享自己的穿搭，累積了非常多的追蹤者而名利雙收。業者也會透過部落客來作產品介紹，以較不商業化的方式，分享實際的經驗。當然目前許多專業的部落客，是接受商品推薦的邀約，撰寫文章來賺取費用，再透過眾多的粉絲分享以及口耳相傳；不管是何種方式，品牌都能增加能見度。

職場上實況對談的一問二答　 Track 45

除了部落客之外，化妝師也是公關需要培養的人脈之一。（Networking with fashion bloggers and make-up artists can help achieve coverage online.）。原因是雜誌拍攝或人物專訪，你會需要好的化妝師來呈現好的畫面。現在化妝師也是一個很熱門的行業，化妝師在網路上宣傳作品的同時，也是品牌曝光的機會。以下是 Amilia 與部落客 Blogger 與化妝師 Stylist 之間的問答：

Question 1

Ⓑ Hey, Amilia. Thank you for sponsoring my picnic photo shoot on my blog. I have always been a fan of your brand. The simplicity and the fine tailored details goes with everything. Are these the pieces that you are recommending to me for the photo shoot?

嗨，愛蜜莉亞，謝謝妳贊助我部落格上的主題野餐拍攝。我一直都是貴品牌的粉絲喔！簡單的線條和細緻的剪裁，非常容易跟其他服裝搭配。這些就是妳要推薦給我的衣服嗎？

Possible answer 1

Ⓐ Yes, they are! Considering your healthy skin tone, I prepared our spring line off shoulder yellow ruffle lace top with a matching shorts. It will accentuate your complexion and make you look chic on a sunny picnic. Here is a pair of nude leather flats with man-made soles that are comfortable and classy for an outdoor event.

是的！考慮到妳健康的膚色，我準備了粉黃色露肩荷葉邊蕾絲上衣和同款的短褲。它會襯托妳的膚色，讓妳在充滿陽光的野餐上看起來很別緻。這雙手工鞋跟的膚色皮革平底鞋，方便行走，很適合優雅的戶外活動。

Possible answer 2

Ⓐ Yes, we have laid out 4 pieces for you. I have a romantic spring picnic in mind, so I paired a floral print bohemian dress and a fringe bag for your look. Since your outfit gives out a very free spirit, I thought a pair of our stylish leather boots would make you seem more down to earth. Lastly, I threw in a tweed jacket for you in case the weather gets chilly. You are going to look flawless.

是的，我們為您準備了 4 個物件。我想像一個浪漫的春日郊遊，所以找了印花波西米亞長裙，搭配流蘇包款的風格。衣服看起來自由奔放，所以我搭配了我們的時尚皮靴，讓妳看起來比較平易近人。最後，我也準備了花呢外套讓妳保暖。妳會看起來完美無瑕。

Question 2

🅢 **Thank you for always supporting me in my career. I have lost count of how many make-up sessions I have cooperate with you on. As for the photo shoot today, what kind of make-up style are you looking for?**

嗨！愛蜜莉亞，謝謝妳一直支持我的事業，我根本記不得我們梳化妝配合過多少次了。今天拍攝主題，妳想要什麼樣的化妝風格呢？

Possible answer 1

🅐 You are welcome. You have been a great help in my career as well. Your make-up technique is by far the best I have ever seen. We are launching a black and white clothing line, so the models should wear clean and minimal make-up. The hair should be pulled back and sleek like a runway show.

你太客氣了，你也一直在我的職業生涯上有很大的幫助，你的化妝技術是到目前為止，我所見過最好的。我們現在要推出黑色系和白色系的服裝系列，所以對於模特兒我希望她們的妝容乾淨，幾近裸妝。髮型應該梳得很俐落，像時裝秀一樣。

Possible answer 2

Ⓐ The feeling is mutual and I have the best time working with you! The clothing line is inspired by the classic aesthetic 40's style, so I want big wavy hair with rosy lips. No long lashes will be needed; I want a natural and outgoing look for the models. They should appear confident and a little bit sexy.

我跟你有一樣的想法，跟您合作一直都很開心！這次的服裝靈感來自於 40 年代的復古風格，所以我想要大波浪的髮型以及漂亮的玫瑰色嘴唇。不需要假睫毛，我想要模特兒盡量自然和活潑的樣子。她們應該顯得自信又帶有一點點性感。

特助補給單字

tailor *v.* 剪裁

tone *n.* 色調

ruffle *n.* 皺摺

complexion *n.* 膚色

minimal *adj.* 極少的

 秘書特助對答技巧提點

I have a romantic spring picnic in mind, so I paired a floral print bohemian dress and a fringe bag for your look.

⊃ Pair 配對。與某物搭配可以用 with 來做連結。例 1：They paired Titi and Meimei in a group, hoping they will finally get along.（他們把蒂蒂和莓莓配在同一組，希望她們最終會可以和平相處。）例 2：Grilled steak paired with Cabernet Sauvignon is a match made in heaven.（烤牛排和卡本內蘇維濃紅酒是天造地設的一對。）

⊃ Look 一般常見的用法是動詞用法，是看的意思。文中是名詞的用法，代表穿衣風格或是穿著樣式的意思。Look 當名詞來用也有眼神的涵義。例 1：To complete the look of the season, you need a floral romper, a pair of platform shoes, sunglasses and a big hat.（要完成本季最流行的穿搭，你需要花朵連身褲、厚底高跟鞋、太陽眼鏡和一個大帽子。）例 2：Don't give me that look; you are the one who forgot the wallet!（不要給我那種眼神，忘記帶錢包的人是你耶！）

 秘書特助經驗分享

　　時尚公關總很容易認識充滿藝術天分的人，例如化妝師、造型師、髮型師、部落客或攝影師，讓超時工作的行業帶來不少樂趣。跑趴的時候要多帶一些名片，手機要充飽電，這些身上滿是創意的人，記得要留聯絡方式，對宣傳品牌一定幫得上忙！

參加設計師派對與經營人脈

Participating in designers' party and networking

 秘書特助工作內容介紹

　　經常出席時尚派對，是為了認識更多在媒體上有影響力的人物，比方說雜誌社的主編、記者、名媛、部落客或是其他數位媒體人，因此需要盛裝出席的派對，其實也是媒體報導豐富刊物內容的方法之一。提供大家互相認識，促進異業結合的可能性，亦為這些派對的隱藏性目的。有的設計師會自己辦發表會與媒體餐會，身為時尚公關的你，得把握機會出席喔！這不但是見習活動的好機會，也可以認識媒體，順便探探競爭對手的訊息。參加時尚派對，絕對是公關工作的美好之一啊！

職場上實況對談的一問二答　⊙ Track 46

很多不正式的 after party，總是可以認識一些傑出的藝術家或是新銳設計師，也許有機會為品牌添增供應商或是好員工也說不定。Attending designers' parties after working hours will always bring you good surprises. 以下是 Amilia 與設計師 Jocelyn 的問答：

Question 1

J Hey, Amilia! You came! Look at all these people here; I don't even know half of them. Thank you for bringing your friends from the media. Now I have a couple of interviews to get to. So what do you think of my fashion show?

嗨，愛蜜莉亞！妳來了！看看這些人，甚至有一半以上的人我都不認識！感謝妳介紹媒體朋友給我，現在我還有幾個專訪邀約。你覺得我的時裝秀怎麼樣呢？

Possible answer 1

A Are you kidding? Your after party is always full of interesting people. I think I met one of my closest friends at your party! I adore your kick-off party idea with DJ and cocktails; it really gets people in the mood to anticipate the runway show.

你在開玩笑吧？你的秀後派對總是充滿了有趣的人，我現在很好的朋友也是在你的派對上認識的。我喜歡你揭開序幕的

音樂和雞尾酒派對的想法，那讓我們更期待接下來的時裝秀。

Possible answer 2

🅐 Why would I miss a jaw-dropping party? Look at the on site portrait studio and poker tables; I think all of your guests are having a good time in your wonderland. I like the long boots and ponchos especially; you can either go casual or pair them with a fancy top, either way the design just works.

我怎麼會錯過一個充滿驚喜的聚會呢？看現場的小型攝影棚和橋牌桌，我想所有的來賓都會在你的樂園裡玩得很開心。我特別喜歡長筒靴和披風，你可以走休閒風或搭配華麗的上衣，這設計就是很耐看。

Question 2

🅹 **This is my first attempt at showcasing my design in a poolside brunch. What do you think? I am worried that it's too causal, but I just can't resist promoting my brand with these swan pool floats. I think they will create a frenzy in social media.**

嗨！愛蜜莉亞，這是我第一次嘗試用游泳池畔早午餐的方式，展示品牌設計。妳覺得怎麼樣？我擔心它會過於休閒，但我就是無法抗拒用這些可愛的大型天鵝漂浮游泳圈來宣傳我的品牌，我認為他們應該會造成社交媒體狂潮。

Possible answer 1

🅐 I think it's worth a shot. Any product launch is a way to get the media's attention. This pool brunch event is definitely one that will be talked about.

我認為這得確值得一試，任何產品的推廣都是用來獲得媒體的關注。這個池畔早午餐絕對會是一個被討論的話題。

Possible answer 2

🅐 Since you are launching summer attire, I don't see any contradiction in the poolside brunch. I have been to many fancy parties that I wanted to leave within 10 minutes. Now I kind of want to change into the bathing suit that you gave us and lay on one of the swan floats. This is a great party, Jocelyn!

既然你是推出夏裝，我不覺得在游泳池畔早午餐有什麼矛盾的地方。我去過很多高級的派對，那些我 10 分鐘就想走人了。而你現在這個派對讓我有點想要換上你剛才送我們的泳衣，躺在天鵝泳圈上放空。喬斯琳，這個派對真的很成功。

特助補給單字

anticipate *v.* 期待

portrait *n.* 肖像

attempt *v.* 嘗試

frenzy *n.* 狂熱

秘書特助對答技巧提點

I adore your kick-off party idea with DJ and cocktails; it really gets people in the mood to anticipate the runway show.

➲ Kick off 通常是用來形容球賽開球，或是活動的開始。現在時尚週除了 after party 之外，連時尚週開始前也會舉辦開始派對（kick-off party）。它也有動詞的用法，例 1：Let's have a press conference to kick off this marketing campaign.（讓我們舉辦新聞發表會，來展開這次的行銷活動。）例 2：I am going to kick off my bachelorette party by going to Hawaii for a week with my girls.（我將和我的好姐妹們飛到夏威夷一個禮拜，來展開我的婚前派對。）

I don't see any contradiction to the poolside brunch.

➲ Contradiction 矛盾、抵觸，因為通常在討論兩者之間的矛盾點，所以 contradiction 後面也常接介系詞 between（在……之間）。例 1：There was a contradiction between her words and what actually happened.（她的話和實際發生的事情間有點矛盾）。例 2：Eating meat is in contradiction to his religion.（吃肉違反他的宗教。）

秘書特助經驗分享

　　打扮得漂亮體面去參加時尚派對，是公關這個工作很令人羨慕的原因之一。如果會前的打扮、參加派對與在派對上與不認識的人聊天，不是你擅長的事，甚至有點痛恨，那你得仔細考慮，公關這行業是否適合你。認識各行各業的人，嘗試在其中找出連結，並運用在品牌宣傳上，基本上就是公關工作的縮影。

MEMO

UNIT
23 歐美時尚週

Fashion weeks in fashion capitals

 秘書特助工作內容介紹

　　國際的大型時裝週有巴黎時尚週（Paris Fashion week）、紐約時尚週（NYFW）、倫敦時尚週（London fashion week），還有米蘭時尚週（Milan fashion week），一年都會各有兩次發表會。在這個盛會上，時尚界的重要人物都會出現，使出渾身解數穿出自己心目中最耀眼的時尚穿搭。每年的潮流與街頭風格，也都會受時尚週的影響而改變。如果你是時尚界的一員，你就算沒有辦法參加，你也得關注這些活動，每季的流行元素變化多端，你一不注意就會被排除在外了。身為時尚公關，瞭解潮流你才能把工作做好。

職場上實況對談的一問二答　　⊙ Track 47

時尚週的入場券一票難求，如果你不從事時尚產業相關的行業，你是無法接近時尚週的。通常品牌都會請明星、時尚部落客、雜誌編輯與記者進入會場。你還得與各國的採購與 VIP 客戶競爭位子，因此時尚週對各界的魅力，是可想而知的。以下是 Amilia 與記者 Journalist 之間的問答：

Question 1

🇯 **Hi, Amilia. Thank you for filling me in on the latest news about New York Fashion Week. Could you walk us through a day in fashion week?**

你好愛蜜莉亞，感謝你對紐約時裝週的最新消息，你能帶我們看一天的時裝週嗎？

Possible answer 1

🅰 With pleasure. Well, everyone probably thinks NYFW is all about glamour and fun, which is only partially true. As a publicist, we need to look after every step of the fashion show, from seating to guest list, as well as many obstacles that can prevent the show from running smoothly, such as preventing photographers from breaking into the show without invitation.

這是我的榮幸。對了，每個人都可能認為是 NYFW 充滿魅

力和樂趣,但這只是一部分。作為一個公關,我們需要顧全時裝秀的所有過程,如座位安排到客人名單,以及處理所有阻撓時裝秀順利進行的障礙,如禁止未受邀請的攝影師闖入。

Possible answer 2

A Of course. To be honest, I was nervous about the show, so I couldn't sleep well for the past few days. I need to make sure the lighting, the music and all the guests are settled in before I can see the show. I actually enjoy seating because when you seat two people together that get along well you can capture adorable photos next to the runway.

當然,說實話我很緊張,這幾天都睡不好覺。我需要先確保所有的燈光和音樂,還有把所有的客人都安頓好,才能好好地看秀。我其實很喜歡安排座位;把兩個相處融洽的人安排在一起,你就能捕捉到他們在伸展台邊的可愛身影。

Question 2

E This is a week with busy and hectic schedule, but it's very interesting. And what would you say is your favorite part of the fashion show?

嗨!愛蜜莉亞,這一個星期日程安排雖然繁忙緊張,但仍然覺得很有趣。在時裝秀中,你最喜歡的地方是什麼呢?

Possible answer 1

Ⓐ My favorite part is definitely seeing a fashion show that's pushing the limits, which reminds me why I entered the fashion industry. It's very inspiring and breathtaking when you see a design or a presentation that's cutting edge. It feels like a new species is being uncovered on earth for the first time.

我最喜歡的地方，肯定是時裝秀上挑戰極限的部分，這讓我想起自己進入這行的原因。當你看到新潮的設計或表演時，會深受啟發，而且感到震憾，那就像新的物種第一次在地球上被發現一般。

Possible answer 2

Ⓐ Being a publicist, I think getting the venue ready, the fashion show up and running, getting all the guests seated and leaving with a smile is very rewarding.

作為一個公關，我覺得讓會場準備就緒，確保時裝秀的運行，以及讓所有的客人入座，並帶著微笑離開是非常有益的。

> ■ 特助補給單字

> obstacle *n.* 障礙
>
> break into *ph.* 闖入
>
> hectic *adj.* 忙亂的
>
> venue *n.* 地點

 秘書特助對答技巧提點

Thank you for filling me in on the latest news about New York Fashion Week.

⊃ Fill in 動詞指填滿、補充，而作為名詞則有代替的意思。順帶補充 fill out 雖然與 fill in 的意思很接近，但差異在於 fill out 是用來形容填寫一整張表格，而 fill in 是指填寫某一個空格，或補充一個項目。例 1：Could you fill in the data numbers for me?（你能幫我填好數據資料的部分嗎？）例 2：I need you to fill out the patient information form since you are a new patient here.（今天是你第一次看診，所以我需要你填寫初診基本資料表。）

My favorite part is definitely seeing a fashion show that's pushing the limits, which reminds me why I entered the fashion industry.

⊃ Push the limits 突破、突破極限。例 1：Marathon runners are pushing the limits of human muscle and mentalities.（馬拉松跑者正在突破人體肌肉和心態的極限。）例 2：The design has pushed the limits of our conception of mobile phones.（這個創新的設計超越了我們對手機的既有概念和限制。）

 ## 秘書特助經驗分享

　　參加國際時尚週的門檻非常高，不過如果你是超人氣的時尚部落客，可以考慮申請看看。以倫敦的時尚週來說，部落格每個月訪客流量起碼要 1 萬人次，而且你要有充分的證據，表現出你對倫敦的服裝設計師有高度的興趣與支持度。社群網站約要有 1 萬個總數的追蹤者。他們希望能透過你讓倫敦時尚週更受到矚目。非常會撰寫文章的你，不妨試試！

秘書特助工作內容介紹

　　時尚業是個競爭激烈的環境，在這個產業擔任行銷或公關，你必須將自己轉化為能夠影響潮流的人。無論是透過創新的行銷手法或是人脈關係，你需要成功的創立品牌、創造銷售奇蹟。時尚潮流可以左右大眾的行銷模式與態度，市場提供非常多的選項，你要如何引導消費者到你的店家選購呢？這也是公關時刻要考慮的課題。再來，你要學會量化你的行銷成果，有著漂亮的成績單，讓客戶心甘情願把品牌委託給你操作。

職場上實況對談的一問二答 Track 48

行銷對品牌的貢獻，來自於品牌的知名度，但品牌的培養需要時間，如果不能立即看得出行銷的效果，公關與行銷部的努力很容易被抹滅。因此定期記錄媒體曝光、報導與經由活動產生的客戶人數能夠降低這樣的誤解。以下是 Amilia 與企業負責人 Pyramid 的問答。

Question 1

🅿 **Amilia, I know we don't have sufficient funds each year for you to operate; nevertheless, we would like to see our investment reflect our revenue. What is your opinion about our decreasing sales numbers in the past 2 months?**

愛蜜莉亞，我知道我們沒有足夠的資金每年可為您操作，儘管如此，我們希望看到我們的投資反映了我們的收入。你對我們降低了近 2 個月的銷售數字的看法？

Possible answer 1

🅐 Mr. P, with all due respect, the fashion business is highly competitive. With our minimum ad campaign and limited funds for events, it's a bit difficult to stay on top in the pool of fashion advertising.

P 先生，恕我直言，時尚行業一向競爭激烈，以我們有限的廣告和活動經費，的確很難在充滿時裝廣告的市場浮上檯面。

Possible answer 2

🅐 Mr. P, I understand where you are coming from. Branding takes time and dedication, and with our excellent team efforts, I am asking you to give us a little more time. Last season I focused most of my time nurturing our brand image. Now, I plan to promote our distinctive professional customer services. The 30 years of experience in the industry will put us in an advantaged position.

P 先生，我可以體會你的感受。品牌建立需要時間和全心全力的經營，有著優秀團隊的努力，我要求你再給我們一點時間。上一季我專注我大部分的時間來培養我們的品牌形象，現在我計劃要宣傳我們的獨特的專業客戶服務。30 年的業界經驗將會讓我們處於優勢。

Question 2

🅟 **I produced an independent film to pay tribute to fashion and I am considering whether I should hire a public relations representative. Could you give me a word of advice?**

我製作了一個獨立電影向時尚界致意，我正在考慮是否要聘請公關代表。可以請妳給我一些忠告嗎？

Possible answer 1

🅐 Sure. For a film to have public awareness, I can help you connect to the right audience. What is your goal in making this film? Once we figure out the message you are trying to communicate, then we can spend some time discussing the outreach strategy. I can introduce you to local publicists throughout the country, as well as meet major directors.

好啊，一部電影要受到大家矚目，我可以幫你連接到正確的族群。你製作這部影片的目標是什麼？一旦我們弄清楚你想傳達的訊息，那麼我們就可以花一些時間討論宣傳戰略。我可以介紹全國各地的公關給你認識，當然還有一些著名的導演。

Possible answer 2

🅐 Certainly. I am in alliance with a strong network of publicists; the collaboration will allow your film to be viewed by professional film critics in different countries. I can also assist you in showing the film in major art exhibits and art festivals of your choice. My experience and network will make all the difference in your screening success.

當然可以，我和一些很有影響力的公關組成一個聯盟。我們能幫你把影片交由不同國家的專業影評人觀看。我也可以幫助你進入各大藝術展覽，或是你希望參加展演的藝術節。我的經驗和人脈可以幫助你的大銀幕之路更順利。

reflect *v.* 反映

independent *adj.* 獨立的

alliance *n.* 結盟

critics *n.* 評論家

 # 秘書特助對答技巧提點

Nevertheless, we would like to see our investment reflect our revenue.

○ **Reflect** 反映、反射，在文中的用法是要表達出公司的預算投資，希望能相對的反映在盈餘上。例：**The peaceful lake reflected the beautiful full moon.**（寧靜的湖面照映了漂亮的滿月。）

Certainly. I am in alliance with a strong network of publicists; the collaboration will allow your film to be viewed by professional film critics in different countries.

○ In alliance with 與……結合，或與……聯合。例：We are in alliance with many other major publishers, so if you decide to sign with us, your book promotion will benefit from all our partners.（我們和許多其他重要的出版商結盟，所以如果你決定跟我們簽約，你的新書發表會將在我們所有合作夥伴的通路當中受益。）

秘書特助經驗分享

　　在台灣媒體公關與行銷行業的重要性很容易被低估。所以身為公關，你得經常為自己品牌的媒體曝光做記錄。雜誌上的廣告與報導，當然一定要做剪報或是留一本存檔，並將廣告稿和雜誌封面漂亮地呈現在官網。辦活動的時候全程記錄，活動後要做效益分析和完整的活動報告。重複對主管提出廣告效益的證明，是公關的必經之路啊！

MEMO

Leader 049

時尚秘書英語 (附 MP3)

作　　　者	黃予辰
發 行 人	周瑞德
執行總監	齊心瑀
企劃編輯	饒美君
校　　　對	編輯部
封面構成	高鍾琪

圖片來源	www.shutterstock.com
內頁構成	菩薩蠻數位文化有限公司
印　　　製	大亞彩色印刷製版股份有限公司
初　　　版	2016 年 8 月
定　　　價	新台幣 380 元
出　　　版	力得文化
電　　　話	(02) 2351-2007
傳　　　真	(02) 2351-0887
地　　　址	100 台北市中正區福州街 1 號 10 樓之 2
E - m a i l	best.books.service@gmail.com
網　　　址	www.bestbookstw.com

港澳地區總經銷	泛華發行代理有限公司
地　　　址	香港新界將軍澳工業邨駿昌街 7 號 2 樓
電　　　話	(852) 2798-2323
傳　　　真	(852) 2796-5471

國家圖書館出版品預行編目資料

時尚秘書英語 / 黃予辰著. -- 初版. --臺北
市 : 力得文化, 2016.08
　　面 ；　公分. -- (Leader ; 49)
ISBN 978-986-92856-8-1(平裝附光碟片)

1. 商業英文 2. 會話

805.188　　　　　　　　　　　105012987

力得文化
Leader Culture

Lead your way. Be your own leader!

力得文化
Leader Culture

Lead your way. Be your own leader!